Praise for Joan Hohl

"A compelling storyteller who weaves her tales
with verve, passion and style."
—*New York Times* bestselling author Nora Roberts

"Joan Hohl is a top gun!"
—*New York Times* bestselling author
Catherine Coulter

"Joan Hohl writes romance
that goes straight to the heart."
—*New York Times* bestselling author
Jayne Ann Krentz

"Writers come and writers go.
Few have the staying power, the enthusiastic
following of Joan Hohl. That's talent!"
—*USA TODAY* bestselling author Kasey Michaels

Dear Reader,

Hi once again, friends. Yes, yes, I know. It's been a long time since my last book, some of you may think much too long. I hope! Well, as I am human and not a machine, parts wear out, I run low on fuel and at times need some TLC. Hey! Maybe I am a machine. A machine who needed a part removed recently. I'm recovering, but each passing year adds another to the score, and, sad as I am to admit it, my score is getting pretty high and I'm slowing down.

As you have likely noticed from the back cover, our hero in the story is, yet again, one of the Wolfe family, or Wolfe pack if you will! Any reader who has read any of my BIG, BAD WOLFE series knows the Wolfes are strong, honest men devoted to their profession—the law.

But Tanner is the maverick of the family. He follows his own rules. Tanner is a bounty hunter, and he does very well at it, thank you. Still, he has never broken the law, nor killed a man. And he always works alone.

Until the lovely Brianna knocks on his door…

Thanks for your loyalty all these years. I truly appreciate it.

Best,

Joan Hohl

JOAN HOHL

MAVERICK

Silhouette® Desire

Published by Silhouette Books

America's Publisher of Contemporary Romance

SILHOUETTE BOOKS

ISBN-13: 978-0-373-76827-1
ISBN-10:   0-373-76827-3

MAVERICK

Recent books by Joan Hohl

Silhouette Desire

*Wolfe Waiting #806
*Wolfe Watching #865
*Wolfe Wanting #884
*Wolfe Wedding #973
A Memorable Man #1075
The Dakota Man #1321
A Man Apart #1640
*Maverick #1718

*Big, Bad Wolfe

JOAN HOHL

is a *New York Times* bestselling author of dozens of books. She has received numerous awards for her work, including the Romance Writers of America Golden Medallion Award. In addition to contemporary romance, this prolific author also writes historical and time travel romances. Joan lives in eastern Pennsylvania with her husband and family.

For Melissa Jeglinski

For all the patience and understanding
she has shown me.

Thanks, Kid!

One

All things considered, she was a traffic stopper.

Tanner raised a questioning eyebrow at the breathtaking woman standing beyond the threshold of the apartment door he had just opened at the buzz of the doorbell.

"Mr. Wolfe?"

A tingle attacked the base of Tanner's spine. Her voice had the effect of warm honey trickling down the length of his back. Her eyes were the color of brandy, her hair a rich, deep, glossy burgundy wine. Combined, they warmed him as if he'd imbibed the drinks themselves.

"Yes." He was rather proud of the steady, almost bored sound of his voice, when bored was the last thing he was feeling. Hot, yes. Bored, no. He lifted one brow. She stood there, all five foot nine or so, slim and classically beautiful, dressed casually but expensively.

One deep, dark eyebrow arched, mirroring his action, as she asked, "May I come in?"

The tingle he felt grew into a sizzle. Damn, it had been a long time since a woman had had such a strong effect on him at first meeting. Come to think about it, no woman had ever had this strong an effect on him.

"Do you have a name?" He injected a droll note into his voice.

"Brianna Stewart," she answered, extending a slim-fingered hand to him. "Now, may I come in?"

Curious—about the woman's courage in entering the apartment of a stranger and about several other things—he took her hand, repressed a shiver, then nodded and stepped back, swinging the door wide as he did so.

"Thank you." Head high, spine straight as an arrow, she walked past him into the neat-as-a-pin living room, her stride relaxed, easy. The late-morning sun's rays slanting through the wide window struck fiery lights off her slightly-redder-than-auburn hair.

"What can I do for you, Ms. Stewart?" he asked. Other than sweep you up and carry you to my bedroom. Telling himself to grow up, he repressed the errant thought.

"May I sit down?" She made a graceful move of one hand to indicate his favorite plush leather recliner.

"Yeah, sure." What else could he say? "Would you like a cup of coffee?" He wasn't about to impart the information that it was the first pot he'd brewed since rolling out of the sack a half hour before she rang his chimes, so to speak. Hell, his hair was still damp from his shower.

"I'd like that, yes, thank you." She smiled.

He suppressed a groan. As slight and polite as her smile had been, it dazzled his senses. What in blazes was wrong with him? he chided himself. She was just another woman. Okay, another gorgeous woman. Wasn't she?

"You're welcome. It'll only take a minute." Avoiding his mental question and telling himself to pull it together, Tanner escaped into the kitchen. Well, he had hoped to escape.

She followed him into the room. "I hope you don't mind, but we can talk in here just as well."

That's easy for you to say. Keeping the thought to himself, where it belonged, Tanner said, "No, I don't mind. Have a seat." He flicked a hand at the retro yellow-and-white chrome-and-Formica kitchen set. "Would you like something with your coffee…some cookies, a muffin, a scone?" Me?

Knock it off, Wolfe.

Sliding onto a plastic-covered chair, she started to shake her head but hesitated, saying, "What kind of scones do you have?"

"Blueberry," he said, removing two diner-type mugs from a wall cabinet.

"Yes, I would. Thank you again." She smiled as if amused at herself. "Blueberry is my favorite."

Damned if her full-blast smile didn't cause a ripple along his nervous system. Lord, the woman was lethal. There was no way he'd admit to her that blueberry was his favorite, too. Even though it was likely obvious, as that was what he had to offer. "Want it warmed?"

"Yes, please." She dazzled him with another smile.

Tanner grabbed two scones into paper napkins, shoved them into the micro and pressed the buttons for twelve seconds. He set the steaming mugs on the table while the micro hummed. The timer beeped while he was setting a carton of milk, a sugar bowl and two spoons on the table.

"Want butter or jam on that?" he asked, going to retrieve the pastries.

She shook her head, swirling the smooth red mass around her shoulders. On the spot, Tanner decided he loved red hair. It was a bit of a surprise, as he had always thought he preferred blondes...even though he didn't consider himself much of a gentleman.

Settling his six foot four inch frame opposite her, he bluntly got to the point. "Okay, now, what brings you to Durango, and what can I do for you?" he said, certain she wanted something from him. The question was, what?

"I want you to find a man for me," she said, her voice calm, almost serene.

What's wrong with *me?* Tanner didn't give

voice to that thought, either. He knew what she meant. "Why?"

Her voice went hard. "Because he needs to be found."

He smiled—almost. "Why, and by whom?"

Her eyes went as hard as her tone. "By my sister, my father, my mother, me and the law."

Now they were getting somewhere. "The law?" Right up his alley. "For what?"

She drew a deep breath, as if to contain a long-simmering anger. "For the rape and murder of one young woman and the attempted rape of another."

"Who sent you to me?"

Brianna raised her eyebrows. "You are a very well-known bounty hunter with an excellent reputation."

"Uh-huh." This time he did smile, wryly, repeating, "Who sent you to me?"

"Your cousins."

He gave her a bored look. "Honey, I have a lot of cousins. Give me some names."

She exhaled a weary-sounding, much-put-upon sigh. "Matt and Lisa."

"Ah, the Amazon twins." He smiled fondly at the memory of his six-foot, gorgeous, only female cousins, the former cop, Matilda, called Matt, and the legal eagle, Lisa. His smile vanished as quickly. "How do you know them?"

"Lisa's my lawyer. She introduced me to Matt," she explained. "But I already knew your mother. She was my history professor in college."

The fond smile hovered once more, while his eyebrows rose in question. "You're from Sprucewood?" It was his hometown in Pennsylvania, before he'd moved out west to Colorado. His mother, the history fanatic, taught the subject at Sprucewood College. His father was chief of the Sprucewood Police.

"No." She shook her head before clarifying. "Not really. I'm from the, er, suburbs."

Tanner wondered about the slight hesitation but let it pass for the moment. "And the man you want found is Jay Minnich. Right?" Before she could respond, he said, "Are you the attempted-rape victim?"

"No." She set her hair rippling again with a sharp shake of her head. "My younger sister, Danielle. The young woman he murdered was Dani's best friend."

"So I read." Tanner nodded.

"Will you find him for us?" Her soft voice held a tinge of pleading. "There's a bounty," she quickly added.

"I know—ten grand." His tone was dismissive, as though ten thousand dollars was nothing. "Posted by your father, the founder and president of Sprucewood Bank."

She frowned at his tone but responded mildly. "Yes, but my father has raised the bounty."

"When?" Surely Tanner would have heard about the bounty being raised if it had been announced. It hadn't.

"Now."

"Say again?" He felt he had somehow missed something.

A small, slightly superior smile touched her soft mouth. "Let me explain."

"Explain away," he invited, raising his mug to his lips and staring intently at her over the rim.

"Dani is an emotional wreck." Her voice was low, sad. "Ever since the…awful events, she has withdrawn into herself. She's terrified that terrible man will come back, find her and kill her, as she was the one who identified him. She won't go out of the house…ever." She paused to sigh before continuing. "In fact, she seldom leaves her bedroom, which she keeps locked at all times. Even her family members have to identify ourselves before she'll open the door. She locks it again after we enter."

"That's too bad," Tanner said sincerely. "It's a horrible experience for any woman to go through, especially a woman her age." Having read everything about the case, Tanner knew the girl was not long out of her teens. And he knew, as well, the woman seated opposite him was a few years older.

"Yes." Brianna paused a minute, then went on. "Although we feel hopeful the law will eventually find this monster, for Dani's peace of mind we want him found and incarcerated as soon as possible. That's why my father entrusted me with finding the best bounty hunter and offering a higher bounty."

From information he had gleaned here and there, Tanner suspected the felon was holed up some-where in the Rocky Mountains, a big territory to scour. Although recently there had been a rumor the man had been spotted in and around Mesa Verde and the San Juan mountain range. That was still a lot of ground to cover. Tanner had previously con-sidered hunting down the man, but he had been bone-tired from his last hunt. Still, he could always use the cash. But then, who couldn't?

"How much higher?" he finally asked, a thread of skepticism in his voice.

Her soft voice hardened. "A million dollars."

A cool mil was worth a man's time needed to comb through that rugged terrain, however tired, Tanner decided. The thought of a million bucks was enough to reenergize a man. If that made him ruthless, tough. Nice guys seldom wound up catching the badasses. Hell, even cops had to be ruthless at times. He should know; there were enough of them in his family.

"Well?" A mixture of anxiety and impatience strained her voice and expression. "Will you accept the job?"

"Yeah," he said in flat tones. "I'll go scour the mountains for him."

"Good." She exhaled the breath he couldn't help noticing she was holding. "I'm going with you."

For a moment Tanner was on the verge of ex-ploding, showering her with heated refusals. Instead he let loose a roar of ridiculing laughter.

"I don't think so," he said when his laughter subsided. "I'm not babysitting a rich man's daughter in stilettos as she traipses around those mountains."

Tapping the toe of one stiletto-clad foot, Brianna smiled serenely. "Mr. Wolfe, I don't need a babysitter, thank you. I can take care of myself."

"Yeah, right," he mocked her. "In a fine restaurant or an upscale dress shop. Go home to Daddy, baby," he advised. "I hunt alone."

"I don't think so," she shot back at him. "This time there'll be two hunters in the mountains."

Tanner laughed again.

He should've kept his mouth shut.

Brianna sat ramrod straight across from Tanner Wolfe, her coffee and scone cooling, her gaze meeting his stare for glaring stare. There was no way he'd keep her from going hunting with him. Not when her sister's life and happiness depended on capturing her offender.

Brianna wasn't about to sit idly by and leave that to someone else. She had to take action, be a part of the hunt. It was the way she had been raised and the way she lived her life. One put family above all else. Besides, back in Pennsylvania, at the university, that was the way she ran her research library. Always in charge.

It didn't matter that this wasn't as routine as finding obscure facts for a student's thesis or a professor's lecture. This was a life-or-death situation—and it could very well be her own death.

But she was doing it for Dani.

She gave Tanner her iciest stare and waited for his reply.

"I said no, Ms. Stewart." His eyes had narrowed to glittering dark stones. "I won't be responsible for anyone else. I always hunt alone."

"Why?" Deliberately, with a show of nonchalance, she raised her mug and took a deep swallow. "I would think two hunters would be better than one."

"Why? Because you're a woman, that's why."

A woman indeed. Brianna fought back a sneer. The man's arrogant, superior tone was getting to her. "I've heard there are women bounty hunters."

"There are," he said, raising his own mug and draining it. "But they're tough, not sleek and pampered daddy's darlings." His smile was no longer gentle. "Even so, I won't hunt with any one of them, either."

Now Brianna was getting more than annoyed. She set down the mug to keep from flinging it at his thick head. She detested a condescending male attitude. She drew a deep breath before educating him.

"Mr. Wolfe, I don't know about women bounty hunters, but this 'daddy's darling' knows how to take care of herself. My father, an avid hunter, began teaching me about firearms when I was twelve. I've followed him up one mountain and down another. I've trekked beside him in Africa.

And, although I hunt with a camera, I'm an expert shot with both a rifle and a handgun."

"I'm impressed."

He sounded bored.

Damn him, Bri thought, gritting her teeth to keep from screaming at him. "I'm not finished," she said, her voice tight. "I've also had training in the martial arts and Krav Maga. I know how to defend myself."

"I'm glad to hear it." He didn't sound at all glad; his voice carried a thread of impatience. "A woman should be trained to protect herself. But that changes nothing. I still hunt alone."

He was a Wolfe, all right, spelled *wolf,* pure alpha male, self-contained and confident. That was certain despite his appearance.

Not that there was anything wrong with the way he looked. It was just that he didn't seem to fit the rest of the Wolfe clan.

Her friends Lisa and Matt were twins, blonde and gorgeous. Bri had never met their parents, but she had met their father's brother, the Sprucewood chief of police, and she had seen pictures of several of the other Wolfes, uncles and cousins. They were all tall, blond and handsome. She had not seen a picture of this particular Wolfe cousin.

Tanner Wolfe was different from the rest. For one thing, he didn't have the same blond hair as the others. While he was every inch as tall as the rest of his family, that's where the resemblance ended.

The other Wolfe males, while handsome, looked the role of tough law-enforcement officers.

The only descriptive word for this Wolfe that had flashed through her mind when he'd opened the door was *saint*. Tanner Wolfe had the face of a saint, with soft brown eyes and a gentle, if possibly deceptive, smile. His hair was wavy and shoulder-length, light brown with red-gold highlights, very clean and shiny.

When she'd first seen him, he had literally taken her breath away. Her immediate thought was that she had rung the wrong doorbell. This saintly-looking soft-eyed man could not be a tough bounty hunter.

But he was. In spades.

Tanner Wolfe was believed by many to be one of the very best criminal hunters in the business.

Incredible.

"Did you fall asleep?"

His softly voiced question drew Bri from introspection. Blinking, feeling foolish, she naturally bristled.

"No, of course not," she denied too strongly, but she sure wasn't about to tell him she'd been doing an inventory of his attractive male attributes. Nor that she'd felt an immediate physical attraction to him.

"Then what were you doing?" Amusement now tinged his soft voice, irritating Bri enough to blurt out the truth—or at least the partial truth.

"I was wondering how someone who looks as nice as you could be so intractable."

"Intractable?" He laughed.

The sound did funny things to her insides, making them kind of quiver. She didn't like the sensation.

"Yes, intractable," she said. "You know, you're being unreasonable by refusing to let me go with you."

"Unreasonable?" He was no longer laughing. In fact, he scowled at her. "Tracking a man is hard, dangerous work."

Bri heaved an impatient sigh. "So is tracking a wild boar or a rogue tiger. But I've tracked both. I'm not a fool, Mr. Wolfe. I'm fully aware of the danger."

"In that case, run along home to Daddy and let me do what I get paid to do."

"No." Sliding back her chair, Bri stood up. "Let's just forget it. I'll find another hunter, one who will allow me to go with him."

"No." Tanner literally sprang out of his chair. "I'm telling you it's not safe."

"And I'm telling you I can take care of myself, possibly even help you." Bri raised her chin, tilting it at a defiant angle. "And I'm telling you I am going—with you or without you. It's up to you, Mr. Wolfe."

"You really are a spoiled brat, aren't you?" he said, his soft voice sounding edgy with frustration and anger. His eyes and mouth were hard. The saintly appearance was gone now, replaced by the hunter.

"No," she calmly denied. "I'm really not. What I am is confident of my abilities and determined to help catch this monster." She drew a deep breath, steeling herself for the blast of fury she expected him to hurl at her. "I'll say it once more—I am going, either with you or with another hunter."

He didn't speak for long seconds, staring at her with narrowed eyes, as if warning her to be careful. His look was absolutely deadly.

Gritting her teeth, Bri managed to hold his gaze, her pulse racing, her heart thumping. She felt like running but stood firm, resolute.

Bri had never allowed any man to intimidate her. Damned if she'd back down from this one, even if he did scare the breath from her body. "A woman."

"What?" Although she had thought Tanner's stare couldn't possibly become any more fierce, it did. "What's that supposed to mean?"

Bri managed a halfway credible shrug. "I mean, I'll look up a woman hunter."

"You will not go after that killer with a woman hunter."

"I'll go with whom I please," she said, her voice calm, resigned.

Although his eyes flashed with anger, he exhaled a quiet sigh of concession. "Okay, you win. I'll take you with me. But I'll have one thing understood before we go any further with this."

"And that is?" Bri had a hard time containing her sense of victory, along with a thrill of excitement.

"I give the orders."

"But—"

"And you will follow them, at once and without protest or question."

Bri went stiff with outrage. Just who did this guy think he was? she railed in silent frustration. Unable to keep her feelings inside, she shot back, "I am not a child to be ordered around. Who do you think you are?"

"I'm the bounty hunter you want or you wouldn't have sought me out in the first place." He smiled, stirring all kinds of emotions inside her. His gaze skimmed her from head to toe, flooding her body with heat. "Just for the record, I'm well aware you're not a child. However, those are my demands."

Defeat was a bitter pill to swallow, but Bri knew she had little choice. She had deliberately sought him out, and not only on the advice of her friends or his cousins.

Bri was thorough in everything she did. She had done her research. She had pulled the information that not only was Tanner considered one of the best bounty hunters around, many believed him to be *the* best at finding his man in rough terrain like mountains.

"All right," she reluctantly agreed. She thought she should feel steam spewing from her ears; instead she felt…protected? She gave a mental shake of her head. No, Tanner Wolfe wasn't feeling protective of her; he was very likely feeling superior.

"Good." He flicked a hand at the table. "Have a seat. We've got a lot of plans to go over."

Wary but resigned, Bri slid onto the chair she had vacated moments before. She picked up the mug, took a sip, made a face and set it down again.

"That's gotta be cold." He grabbed the mug along with his own and turned away. "I'll get us refills." He raised his eyebrows. "What about your scone?"

Bri shook her head. "No, thank you. It's fine this way." Raising the pastry to her mouth, she took a bite. "It's very good."

"Whatever." Shrugging, he turned away.

Chewing another bite of the scone, she watched him, studying him from the rear. It was a very nice rear, narrow, firm and taut. His back and shoulders weren't bad, either, broad and muscular, not in a pumped-up way, but more lean and rangy.

Mugs refilled, Tanner returned to the table, giving her another chance to more closely examine the front of him. That was even better.

His flat, muscled chest veed to a slim waist. His legs were long, straight, his thighs nicely straining the denim of his jeans as he arranged his tall frame in the chair. He regarded her in calm, watchful silence.

Quiet and composed, his features appeared sculpted from marble, sharply delineated. His nose was straight, cheekbones high, jawline defined, square and hard, as if the sculptor had carved it lovingly. If it weren't for those soft eyes and that tender smile, he'd look like a statue. That tiny flare of excitement flashed inside her again. Why? The question hammered at her mind. Bri couldn't find the answer, and that seriously bothered her.

"What are you staring at?" His quiet voice jolted her out of her reverie.

Damn, once again he'd caught her brooding, staring. What in the world was the matter with her? she chastised herself. She had never been so strongly affected by any man. The closest she had ever come to feeling so drawn to a man had been a disaster, for he had proven to be a handsome, charming son of a bitch, a practiced user of young, susceptible women. At the time, she had been both.

"You," Bri admitted, but that was all she intended to admit. "I'm trying to figure you out."

He grinned. "How are you making out?"

"Not too well," she said, deliberately grinning back at him. "You're not easy to read."

"Don't feel bad," he said, growing serious. "I can't figure you out, either. You're sure not what you appear to be."

Bri raised her brows. "How do I appear to be?"

He studied her a moment. "My first impression of you was of a beautiful woman, very well dressed, well-bred and educated."

Despite her suspicion of easy compliments—the SOB had been extremely easy with them—Bri felt her cheeks grow warm, flushed not only by his

words but by the open admiration in his eyes. "I—
I don't know—"

Tanner silenced her with a quick shake of his
head. "Don't get all flustered. I doubt you'll be as
pleased with my opinion of how you're different
from my snap impression."

Bri raised her mug to her lips to sip at the hot
brew, looking relaxed, while in fact she was steeling
herself for whatever he said next. "Go on." How in
the world she had managed a cool tone, Bri hadn't
a clue.

"I think you have been spoiled rotten," he said
with blunt honesty. "You want what you want,
when you want it. I read you as self-centered, self-
confident and too damned sure of yourself."

Why Tanner Wolfe's assessment of her person-
ality should hurt her, she couldn't imagine, but hurt
it did, like the very devil. Odd, usually she wasn't
so sensitive to anyone else's opinions of her. Since
the episode with the silver-tongued weasel, she
thought she had grown a thick skin.

"Now you want to take a shot at me?"

"Of course," Bri said. "But first I'd like to know
how you managed to come to that conclusion in
such a short time with me."

"Easy." Tanner laughed. It sounded relaxed,
genuine. "I recognized the traits because they're
very similar to my own." He paused to laugh again.
"The only difference is I'm not beautiful."

Two

"You're spoiled?" She couldn't help laughing, thinking he was wrong on one point. He *was* beautiful, just in a different, masculine way.

"Sure," he answered, laughing with her. "I have great parents. While instilling morals, values, ethics, good behavior and good housekeeping skills into their sons, they also spoiled the hell out of us. In a good way," he quickly added, grinning.

"You have two brothers, both older than you, right?" she asked, although she knew the answer.

"Yeah." He nodded. "Justin's the oldest, now thirty-two. Then Jeffrey, thirty. And lastly, yours truly, twenty-nine." He grinned again. "There's also a slew of cousins."

"So I've heard." She grinned back at him.

"How old are you?"

Well, no one would ever accuse him of being hesitant. The thought brought a smile to her lips. "I'm twenty-seven."

"You're too young to risk your life traipsing around in the mountains, looking for a killer."

Bri rolled her eyes while heaving a sigh. "I believe we've already plowed that field, Mr. Wolfe. I'm going, period."

"I know, but I had to try one more time." His sigh was heavier than hers. "And the name's Tanner. It would get pretty tiresome hearing Mr. Wolfe over and over for who the hell knows how long."

"Okay…Tanner," she agreed. "My friends call me Bri."

"That's too bad." He smiled at her startled look. "I like Brianna better. It's a lovely name and fits you perfectly. Like you, it's classy."

Bri grew warm with pleasure. He thought she was beautiful and classy? Though many men before him had called her beautiful, his compliment left her speechless for a long moment. Finally she found her voice, if rather weak and a bit breathless.

"Thank you," she murmured, feeling herself grow warmer. "That was very nice of you." Oh, gag me, she thought, disgusted with the inanity of her response.

"You're welcome." Tanner's lips twitched, betraying his urge to grin.

She didn't blame him. She joined him, laughing easily at herself. "Pretty lame, huh?"

He shook his head. "No, surprising. I would have thought you'd be used to compliments."

"Well, yes," she said. "But—"

"But what?" His eyes gleamed with a teasing light.

"Oh, let's just forget it," she said, certainly not for a moment about to admit he flustered her simply because she felt a physical attraction to him. A strong attraction.

"Why?"

"What do you mean, *why?*" She frowned. "Because it's getting silly, that's why."

"Too bad." He sighed. "I thought it was just getting interesting."

Bri rolled her eyes. This man is impossible. Gorgeous, sexy as hell, but impossible. "I think it's time to get down to the business at hand."

He gave another, deeper sigh. Boy, this guy was some actor, Bri thought, struggling against the urge to laugh, amazed at how much she was enjoying their banter, not to mention his company, his appeal. No, let's not go there again, she told herself. As they were going to be spending a lot of time together, it would be in her best interest to avoid thinking about his appeal.

"Are you sulking?" she asked after several long moments—moments in which she had thought about nothing but him.

He smiled. "I never sulk. Children sulk. And, just

on the odd chance you hadn't noticed, I'm a man, not a child."

"Oh, I've noticed," she said, thinking she had noticed too damn much.

He smiled again. "Oh, I've noticed you, too."

His smile was an invitation to sheer temptation. Pull it together, Bri told herself, fighting to control her rapid heartbeat and leaping pulse. You've had one go-round with a sweet-talkin', overconfident type. That encounter was one too many.

But Tanner was an attractive, sexy man. And she was every bit as susceptible as any other normal woman. Why did the devil have to look so angelic?

Tanner smiled—a devilish, suggestive and too damned appealing smile.

Now Bri not only felt warm, she felt hot all over. And tingly. And funny inside. Stop it, she told herself. As if *that* helped.

"Uh…um…business," she said, stumbling a bit over her words—something she had never done. "I really think it's time to get down to business."

"Too bad." Tanner shook his head, looking or trying to look sad. His gleaming eyes gave him away. "But, if you insist, we'll get down to the nitty-gritty."

"I do. And that is?"

"Set a day to leave and gather the supplies needed for this hunt."

"I can leave tomorrow."

"I haven't told you yet everything we'll need to

take with us," he said. "So how can you be ready by tomorrow?"

She shot him an impatient look. "If you'll recall, I did tell you I have been hunting since I was a kid. I know how and what to pack."

"Okay, kid," he said, heavy on the *kid*. "But I think I'll do a list, just to be on the safe side, make sure we're on the same page, so to speak." Getting up, he walked to the counter and pulled open a cabinet drawer. He took out a pencil and a pad of paper, then hesitated, turning his head to glance at her. "More coffee?"

"No, thank you." Bri shook her head and shot a glance at her watch. "How long is this going to take?"

His lifted one brow. "Why? Are you in a hurry?"

"No, but the only thing I did was check in to the hotel and get my room card. I left my stuff with the bell captain and came right here."

"How did you know I'd be here?"

"Lisa told me." She smiled, maybe a bit smugly. "She spoke to your mother last night, who told Lisa you had called and said you had just returned."

Tanner scowled.

Bri rushed to clarify her statement. "Your mother knew I was coming here to try to hire you." She drew a breath and went on more normally. "She told Lisa she would let her know as soon as she heard from you."

"Women." He heaved a sigh and shook his head.

She bristled at his dismissive tone. "What's wrong with women?"

Tanner slid a wry look at her. "Most of the time, like children, they should be seen and not heard."

Stunned, Bri was speechless for a moment. Though sorely tempted to explode all over him, she forced herself to remain calm, icy calm. "Mr. Wolfe, that is the stupidest, most sexist remark I've ever heard. What century are you living in?"

"Honey, I'm right here and now," he said, every bit as calm and icy. "I may not be politically correct, but I'm honest. I'm a women jabber. Simple as that."

"Forget it."

"Gladly. Now…"

"No," she shook her head, sliding her chair back and rising. "I mean forget about finding that poor excuse for a man. I'll hire someone else." Before the last word was out of her mouth, she turned to leave. "Or hunt him myself."

"No, you won't." His voice was sharp with command. "I'm going, with or without you," he repeated her earlier ultimatum back to her. "Now, Brianna, sit down and let's get down to business."

Bri hesitated, telling herself that if she had any sense or pride, she would tell Tanner Wolfe to go to hell, walk out of there and look up another hunter. Her sense must have deserted her, for she sighed and swallowed what was left of her pride. In the final analysis, she was determined Minnich would be caught and she wanted the best mountain hunter. So, still glaring at Tanner, she reseated herself.

"Smart girl." He offered a slight smile. She

refused the offer. Instead he shrugged. "Okay, let's get it done."

Smart girl. Yeah, right. She had caved to the caveman, dammit. She soothed her tattered composure by reminding herself Dani's well-being was worth her pride.

"Guns."

Bri blinked herself out of her musings. "What?"

"You said you had your supplies," he said patiently. "What kind of weapons do you have?"

"Oh." Bri felt flustered and foolish. Telling herself to get with it, keep up with him, prove she was a smart girl, she replied, "I've got a .270 rifle with a three-by-nine scope and a .357 hunting revolver." She arched her brows at his sudden intent expression. "What do you pack?"

"A .30-06 and a 7mm rifle with the same scope, and a .44 mag." He looked impressed. "And you really do pack some heavy-duty heat."

Not as much as you do, she thought, referring not to his weapons but to his body. "I told you I knew what I was doing," she said, working at not sounding too smug or too breathless. "Anything else?"

His lips twitched, evidently amused by her. "Clothes, backpack, sleeping bag?"

"Yes." Now her lips twitched. "All of the above."

He smiled. "Wanna tell me about them? Just a hint?" His smile grew into a grin.

Bri gave a mock sigh, fighting the smile tickling the corners of her mouth. Darn him, why did he have to be so attractive? "I have clothes suitable for mountain terrain, including a ski jacket neatly packed in my backpack, along with other necessities. My sleeping bag is the best available and waterproof. I lay it on a nearly weightless ground sheet. Now are there any other questions?"

"As a matter of fact, there are," he said. "What about food? Have you thought of that?"

This time she gave him a droll look. "Of course I have, but I didn't bring much with me. I figured we could get what we needed here in Durango."

He nodded. "You figured correctly." He pushed the chair back and stood. "Let's get lunch. We'll take my truck."

"Wait a minute," she protested while standing and following him from the kitchen. "Who said anything about lunch?"

"I just did." He shot a glance at the big red-rimmed clock on one wall. "It's nearly one. I'm hungry for something more substantive than a scone. Aren't you?"

"Well, yes," she admitted reluctantly, because she was feeling too attracted to the arrogant Neanderthal. "Why not take separate vehicles?"

Tanner paused, holding open the door for her. "You know your way around Durango?"

She had never even been to Durango, Colorado, before. "Well, no, but—" She was about to mention the restaurant in her hotel, but that's as far as she got before he cut her off.

"That's what I thought. We'll take my truck."

Bri had no intention of doing so. She shook her head. "I want to go to the hotel and freshen up a bit. Give me directions. I'll meet you at the restaurant in a half hour."

The restaurant Tanner had directed her to was done in Western decor, not honky-tonk but with style and ambience. Now, in early afternoon, there were few patrons, so the place was quiet.

"This is very nice," she said to Tanner, seating herself in the chair the host held for her. She smiled at the man. "Thank you."

"Wait till you've tasted the food," Tanner said.

She looked over the long list of dishes offered on the menu. Her glance halted at shrimp and pasta in a light herb dressing. On the spot, she dumped the idea of her normal luncheon salad.

She placed her order when the waitress came, then looked up at Tanner. She felt certain he would order red meat, like a rare steak. He surprised her. A talent he seemingly had in abundance.

"I'll have the pasta, as well, but with chicken."

The server no sooner turned away when a young woman came to an abrupt stop at their table. She was blond, petite and more than pretty. Her big blue eyes sparkled with surprised pleasure. Her teeth gleamed in a brilliant yet sensuous smile.

"Tanner, honey!" Miss Sunshine exclaimed,

moving into his arms when Tanner stood. "I haven't seen you in ages. What have you been up to?"

For some inexplicable reason, everything about the young woman annoyed Bri, from her cooing voice to the possessive way her arms curled around his neck. For a few seconds Bri was even more annoyed at the way Tanner smiled down at the small woman clinging to him. Her annoyance fled with his drawled response.

"Well, Candy, I'm up to the same six feet four inches I was at the last time I saw you...'ages' ago. What has it been—all of a week or two?"

Somehow Bri contained the laughter bubbling up inside her at his reply. And her name! *Candy.* It certainly fit, all right. She was arm candy for hungry males.

The thought sobered Bri. Was Tanner one of the hungry males? She was so startled, so bothered by the very idea of Tanner being that predictable, she almost missed him setting the woman from him and turning to her. She quickly rose.

"Brianna, I'd like you to meet Candy Saunders. She's from back east, too—"

"The Hamptons," Candy was quick to arrogantly insert, rudely cutting Tanner off. All sweetness and light were gone, her eyes and smile calculating as she swept a dismissive glance over Bri.

Looking bored, Tanner rolled his eyes at Bri, a wry smile twitching the corners of his mouth.

"Candy of the Hamptons, meet Brianna Stewart of Pennsylvania."

Candy gave a delicate sniff, obviously not impressed. "How nice. Are you visiting someone here in Durango?" She arched one perfect bleached eyebrow. "One of Tanner's friends, perhaps?"

Bri didn't know whether to laugh or slug the overbearing woman. She did neither, of course. Instead she answered drily, "No, I'm not visiting. I have business with Mr. Wolfe."

"Really?" Both eyebrows went up.

"Yeah, really," Tanner said, now sounding as bored as he looked. "If you'll excuse us?" He indicated a table toward the back. "I think your friend is getting impatient for you to join him."

Candy turned back to him, instantly changing to Miss Sunshine again. "Yes, of course, darlin'," she cooed, raising a small hand to lightly drag her dagger nails down his face. "Toodles," she said, drawing her hand away and wiggling her scarlet-tipped fingers at him. "Call me." Without so much as a glance at Bri, she sashayed away.

"Toodles?" Battling another bubble of laughter sparked by the drama queen, Bri resumed her seat just as the server approached the table with their meals.

"That's Candy," he said, shrugging.

Yes, Bri mused, but did he like candy? Mentally dismissing the oddly disturbing idea, she asked, "A good friend of yours?" The question was out before she could stop herself. Dammit, she didn't give a rip either way…did she?

Tanner saved her from her self-condemnation. "No." He shook his head, setting his long waves rippling, brushing his shoulders. "She's a bit of an airhead, I'm afraid, and calls every man 'darlin'' in that cloyingly sweet voice." He shrugged. "But she can be polite and even amusing at times."

"I see." Bri hid a frown of dissatisfaction by lowering her head to inhale the aroma wafting from the steaming plate the server set in front of her.

The food was delicious. The conversation, which didn't include candy of any sort, ranged from favorite foods to favorite movies to general likes and dislikes. Bri relaxed, let her guard down.

It was a mistake she rarely made.

On leaving the restaurant, feeling mellow—too mellow—she soon realized she had been led down the conversational garden path, so to speak.

"Where are you staying?" Tanner asked as they headed for their vehicles.

"The Strater Hotel. It's lovely."

"Yeah, a landmark, built in 1887." His tone held a tiny note of the proud resident. "You know, Will Rogers stayed there. And Louis L'Amour wrote several of his Western novels while he was staying there."

"He must have stayed a while," she said, smiling at his instructive tone. "Or written very fast."

He grinned.

Bri felt something inside go all squishy. Why did he have to have such a sexy grin? She swallowed a sigh of self-disgust—or was it longing?—and was relieved when they came to her rental SUV. "This one's mine."

"I'm right behind you." He moved his head, indicating the much larger, kick-ass SUV. "I've got some calls to make before I go for the food supplies and some loose ends to tie up tomorrow. Suppose I pick you up the day after tomorrow? I want to get an early start. Is five okay with you?"

In that instant Bri became wary of his intentions. "You *will* be here, won't you?"

At once, his pleasant expression changed, his features growing taut. "Didn't I just say I will?" His voice carried both anger and insult.

"Yes." Bri was not about to apologize. "But I want to be certain you won't take a flit on me."

"A flit…" He shook his head. "What are you getting at? Do you believe—" As he paused, she pounced.

"That you're going to take off on your own, leave me cooling my heels here in Durango?" she finished for him. "Oh, yeah, Mr. Wolfe, that's exactly what I think you might try. I guess I should have listened to your cousins. They warned me you were a loner, a maverick who went his own way alone." He started to speak, but she charged on. "And that's what you intend to do to me, isn't it?"

"Okay, I admit I prefer to do my hunting alone,

as I always have. But I had agreed to your going with me, so why in hell did you get the idea that I was planning to take off without you?" Now Tanner sounded angry, and his features had hardened, turning the saint into the bounty hunter.

Bri wasn't impressed by either his voice or the hard look of him. At least she worked to appear unimpressed. In truth, she was shaken, trembling inside. But that was because she was just as angry.

"Oh, couldn't be because you now seem eager to get rid of me while you get your stuff together, now could it?" She didn't wait for him to ditch the stunned, speechless look, but continued, "It might even have worked except for one minor detail. You forgot that I'm carrying the check."

"I didn't forget a damned thing."

Whoa. If she had thought he was angry before, she was now seeing real anger. More like fury. And furious, Tanner Wolfe was downright frightening.

"Good, because even if I'd have bought into your softening-up routine in the restaurant—" he again opened his mouth to interrupt but she held up her hand, keeping him still while she rushed breathlessly on "—and you skipped off on your own and brought in that bastard, you wouldn't have gotten anything but the original ten thousand bounty."

"Finished?" His cold tone was chilling.

The tremor inside Bri turned into an icy shiver she was hard-pressed to hide from him. "Yes." How she had managed so calm a tone amazed her.

"Feel better for having your little rant?" There was something new and dangerous in his voice that froze the icy shiver solid.

Bri stiffened her spine and raised her chin to a defiant angle. "I was not ranting."

"Coulda fooled me," he drawled. "And there was no softening-up in the restaurant. I guess I'm not too bright, because I thought we were having a nice time getting to know each other." He gave her a quizzical look. "What made you think I was setting you up, anyway?"

How did one explain a feeling, a sudden onslaught of intuition? she asked herself. A hard lesson learned from another man who'd been a pro at stringing along women?

"I'm not quite sure myself," she admitted. "When we were talking, I relaxed, and the next minute I began to feel suspicious." She told herself the sudden feeling had nothing to do with how he had allowed that man-eater Candy to step into his embrace.

At the back of her mind, another unsettling suspicion niggled at her. The suspicion that he might have been in a hurry to send her packing so he could go back to the restaurant to indulge in some after-dinner candy. *Then* he would collect his stuff and head into the mountains without her.

Bri brushed the suspicion off, not about to recognize it. There was no way she would voice it to Tanner. His heavy sigh dissolved her uncomfortable reverie.

"Do you want to spend the next two nights with me?"

Yes, she thought at once. "No," she said in firm denial of her first response.

"Then I suppose you'll have to trust me." He smiled quite like a chess player who had his opponent checkmated. "That is, if you still want to go with me."

"You know I want to go with you," she snapped, angry at him, at herself for stepping so blindly into his game of strategy. "As long as you remember who holds the purse strings."

Tanner shook his head as if in pity for her. "I don't forget details, Brianna, even when they are recited by a spoiled little rich girl."

Bri simmered over his parting shot at her the rest of the day and all through the next, all the while she wandered around, checking out the shops closest to the hotel.

She'd show him what a spoiled little rich girl could do.

Three

Damned if she wasn't wearing killer heels.

Tanner stared in amazement as he brought the SUV to a stop in front of her hotel. It was early, still dark, not so much as a hint of gray on the eastern horizon. But standing in the well-lit entranceway of the hotel, leaning indolently against the brass handrail, he spotted the incongruous heels at once.

At any other time, the so-called shoes—consisting of two narrow straps across her toes and ribbons wound around her ankles, paper-thin soles and those slim, long, spiked heels—would have looked sexy. Worn with jeans and a field jacket over a green camp shirt, they looked ludicrous…and sexy.

Brianna stood there waiting for him, her gear piled next to her left leg, the strap handle of a rifle carrier in her right hand by her side. To his chagrin, her gorgeous mass of auburn hair was tucked away inside a New York Yankees baseball cap. He felt plain, ordinary and underdressed in black jeans, a black leather jacket and sturdy boots. He also had pulled his hair away from his face, tied it with a leather thong at his nape.

Stepping from the SUV, Tanner circled around the back to open the trunk lid. The hotel doorman stashed the gear next to Tanner's. Before he could dip into a pocket to tip the man, Brianna handed him a couple bills and uttered a soft, "Thank you."

"Good morning," Tanner said to her.

"Mmm," she hummed in reply, turning away to get into the front passenger seat.

It would appear she was still ticked off at him. Tanner sighed and slid behind the wheel. Mentally shrugging, he drove away from the hotel, heading out of Durango.

"I love your shoes," he drawled. "I can just imagine you tromping around rough mountainous terrain in them."

She laughed. "I'd hoped you'd appreciate them."

"Oh, I do. They're spectacular, and the color is perfect. Glittery gold straps go great with jeans, field jackets and caps."

"I thought so." She laughed again when he flashed her a grin. "I'm sorry to have to disappoint you, but I won't be wearing them to tromp around any rough terrain. I do have hiking boots with me."

"Aw, gee, that's too bad," he said. "I was looking forward to watching you try to keep up with me." Now the quick look he sent her was glittery with teasing. "Then again, I'll likely still be watching you try to keep up with me."

"In your dreams," Brianna shot back. "What you'll likely be watching is my back."

Tanner couldn't help himself; he roared with laughter. She was so damned sure of herself, so boldly feisty. He also couldn't help but admire her. On the spot, he decided it was probably because she reminded him of himself.

"We'll see," he said, still chuckling.

"Yes, I guess we will." She grew quiet, gazing out through the windshield and side window at the landscape as it changed from mountainous to flatter, barren desert.

"Where are we going?" she asked.

"Not far from Mesa Verde."

"Mesa Verde? I thought you said our quarry was headed deep into the San Juan Mountains."

"What I said was I had picked up a rumor that he was heading there." He spared her a brief glance. "Before I go tearing into the mountains, I want to check out the rumor for myself."

"And who are you going to check out these rumors with—the ghosts of the Indians who lived there?" Her tone held more than a hint of sarcasm.

"Clever," he said, sighing. "Actually, I didn't say we were going to Mesa Verde itself. The rumor I'd picked up was that he had been spotted around Mesa Verde before hightailing it to the mountains. I'm headed for a town where the rumor came from."

"Oh, okay." Brianna was quiet for a moment— a short moment. "I wouldn't mind stopping in Mesa Verde."

Stunned by her startling remark, Tanner nearly lost control of the vehicle. It went off the road, onto the rough shoulder, before he righted it.

"You want to do what? Have a look-see at Mesa Verde?"

"What's wrong with that?"

"Brianna," Tanner said between clenched teeth, "I thought we were out here to search for a rapist/killer, not go on a sightseeing jaunt."

"Well, of course we are," she said, abrading his irritation with her reasonable tone. "I meant someday I'd like to explore the cliff dwellings."

"I'm sorry." In truth, he wasn't at all sorry. "I thought you wanted me to stop today to go crawling around the ruins, and we have no time to waste."

"But you wasted all day yesterday," she protested.

Tanner was on the sharp edge of impatience. "Brianna, I told you I had a lot to do yesterday. Besides having to make some phone calls to tie up a few loose ends, I had to get our food supplies, which I paid for."

She sighed. "Okay, explanation accepted."

"Big of you," he drawled with a bite.

"I know," she said sweetly. "And, of course, I'll reimburse you for the supplies."

"Damned straight you will, honey." His voice had a hard edge he didn't like. Get a grip, Wolfe, he warned himself, before you find yourself without a mission...and the company of the gorgeous but irritating Brianna. As he fully expected, she retaliated.

"Don't go all predator on me. I'm not one of your prey," she shot back at him. "And don't call me 'honey.'"

Predator? She thought of him as a predator? Tanner frowned, not sure whether he wanted to laugh or curse a blue streak. Hell, predators killed their prey, sometimes ate it. He worked hard not to kill his, even the ones who deserved it. And he sure as hell didn't eat his prey, the mere thought revolting.

On second thought, he mused, gliding a quick glance over her body, he wouldn't mind taking a nip of Brianna's satiny-looking skin. The mere thought of tasting her was enough to stir his body. Get your mind back to business, Wolfe, he warned himself, where it's safe. This ultrasuperior, haughty, independent woman was not for tasting, not by him. Damned shame, too.

"I'll make a deal with you," he said, shifting in his seat to relieve an uncomfortable ache in that sensitive area. "You don't call me 'predator,' and I won't call you 'honey.' Deal?"

"Deal," she said, shaking the hand he held out to her.

"How about 'sweetheart'?" he asked, not missing a beat.

"Tanner Wolfe," Brianna cried sternly, before she gave way to laughter. "You're a...a..."

"Devil?" he asked, grinning in delight at having made her laugh instead of berating him.

She raised her hands in surrender. "I give up," she said. "You win—for now."

"Looks like a draw to me," he said as he slowed down. "Good timing, too. We're here."

"So I see," Brianna said, peering through the windshield as he drove into the town. "This is it?"

"Yeah, I know, not much to look at."

"A little larger than other towns I've driven through." She sat forward, as far as the seat belt allowed, to get a better look at the old town.

"Will we be here long enough for me to look for a coffee shop or diner? I need some caffeine."

He parked the SUV in front of a small café. "You want to go traipsing around in those?" He sent a pointed look at her shoes.

Brianna shook her head. "Of course not." She feigned shock. "I couldn't walk around in public in heels and this attire," she went on haughtily. "I'd never dream of committing such a fashion faux pas."

Was she serious? Tanner stared at her for a moment, then laughed.

Brianna laughed with him. "I suppose it is time to change, isn't it?" She flashed a megawatt smile.

Tanner felt something strange inside, a sensation unlike anything he had ever felt before. It was as if there was something coming alive, unfolding deep within him, a current of soft warmth. It was weird. He had experienced heated desire many, many times. But this feeling was different. And it was directly related to the woman seated next to him. He had to swallow, moisten his throat and lips before he even attempted to reply.

"Yes, I suppose it is." He sighed, not even caring if she heard him mutter, "I'm gonna miss 'em." Swinging open the door, he said in the most normal tone he could manage, "I shouldn't be long. Wait for me inside." Stepping out, he motioned to the place. "We might as well have lunch while we're here. Then we won't need to stop again." He raised a brow. "Okay?"

"Fine." She nodded, quickly calling after him as he slammed the door and started away, "I'll need to get in the back to get my boots."

He was lifting the trunk before she had finished. "Yeah, I know."

Releasing the seat belt, she turned to look at him. He grinned, lifting a Western hat and settling it on his head. "I needed this, too."

Bri felt her breath catch with his grin. Darn, what the devil was it about this man? What *something* did he have that no other man had ever possessed to make her heart race, her breath catch, her body go all warm and squishy? Her feelings were even more intense than they had been with— She cut her thoughts short, not even wanting to think that rotten man's name.

"Brianna?"

His voice brought her to her senses. She blinked. "What?" God, she hated the confused, disoriented sound of her own voice.

Tanner frowned. "Are you all right?"

"Yes, of course," she answered crisply. "Why wouldn't I be all right?"

"Beats the hell out of me." He shook his head, still frowning. "All of a sudden you seemed…I don't know…kinda lost or something."

Sure, Bri thought, it was the *something* that got to her. "I was, er, just thinking." Brilliant, Brianna, she chided herself.

"About?" He was frowning again.

About…about…jeez. "About maybe I should just go with you," she said, wincing inside at the inanity and wondering how she could extradite herself from him so she could think clearly.

Fortunately Tanner performed that all by himself with two succinct words. "Think again."

"Huh?" She smothered a groan.

"Brianna, I am not about to take you with me to talk to an informant. Somehow I feel said informant would very likely pretend he didn't even know me. Understand?"

"Yes…yes, of course," she said, feeling more ridiculous by the minute. Looking away from his curious expression, Bri undid the ties around her slim ankles, slipped out of the heels and tossed them into the backseat. "If you would please hand me my pack, I'll change and then go…get some coffee."

"Wouldn't it be easier if you told me where the boots are so I can hand them to you?"

Smart-ass. Bri gritted her teeth to keep from saying the word aloud. "There's a plastic bag attached to my backpack. They're in there."

"Now we're getting somewhere," he drawled, his lips twitching with a smile.

Bri felt her own lips tickle, then she gave way to the laughter bubbling up into her throat. She couldn't explain to herself why it was that when he laughed or smiled, she had to respond in kind.

The trunk lid slammed shut. A moment later he opened her door. "Your slippers, Cinderella." His eyes danced with silent laughter.

"Thank you." She took the sturdy boots from him. "And if you're expecting me to call you Prince Charming, you have a long wait ahead of you."

Tanner laughed out loud, tipped his hat respectfully at her and strolled away.

Now, she thought, *that* was charming. And disarming, thus dangerous to her peace of mind—never mind her libido. Brianna was not a child or a fool. She was a smart, well-educated woman. A woman with the appetites and desires of every healthy human, female or male. She was attracted to Tanner Wolfe, and he was attracted to her. It didn't take a mental giant to figure that out. Human nature would have its way.

Yeah, she mused, pulling on the socks she had jammed into the boots, she had to be careful, on her guard, against herself as well as him. The two of them were going to be spending a lot of time together, closely together, in the mountains.

She had been hurt badly before and was determined she wouldn't be again. She couldn't emotionally afford to get involved with Tanner Wolfe, bounty hunter.

Groaning softly at the very idea, she yanked on the boots, grabbed her shoulder bag and stepped out of the SUV.

Drawing a deep breath, she strode out, determined to put off her ruminations until later. But her stride soon turned into a meandering stroll, while her mind raced ahead with what-ifs.

Bri knew full well the possibilities, knew they narrowed down to one. Her imagination drew a vivid picture of herself and Tanner, their limbs entwined, their mouths fused, his body—

Hold it right there, she told herself, blinking to erase the too-explicit scene from her mind. She was breathing hard and fast. Suddenly aware, she glanced around her to see if anyone had noticed her flushed cheeks, her forehead damp with perspiration. If anyone did, she'd blame it on the noonday sun directly overhead. In her jacket, no wonder she was so uncomfortably warm.

Her breathing slowing but still uneven, Bri turned on her heel to practically run back to where Tanner had parked the SUV in front of the café.

Pulling herself together and shrugging out of her jacket, Bri entered the café, her throat parched. Whether her thirst came from the heat or from her thoughts, she didn't know; all she knew was she needed a cold drink to cool down her fevered mind.

She was seated in a booth, a large glass of ice water set next to a steaming cup of coffee in front of her, working at appearing cool, comfortable and slightly bored, when Tanner entered the café. His sharp gaze locating her at once, he strode to the booth and slid onto the bench across from her. Removing his hat, he set it on the bench next to him. "Hi."

His soft, almost intimate voice sent tingles dancing along her spine.

"Hi, yourself." How Bri had found her impersonal yet friendly tone she hadn't a clue.

"The coffee looks good," he said, indicating her cup with a swift movement of his head. "It's warming up outside."

"I noticed." Bri immediately decided that had to be the biggest understatement of her life. "That's why I asked for the ice water."

"Hmm…and I'm parched."

You're telling me? she thought, taking a quick sip to cool her drying throat.

"Hungry?" she asked, not able to think of anything else to say.

Tanner didn't respond for a few tense seconds, during which he slid a slow, intense look from her face to her waist. "Er, yeah."

He didn't have to say any more; Bri felt his exact meaning in every cell in her body. Oh, boy, she thought, watching his eyes darken as she thoughtlessly wet her dry lips with a glide of her tongue. Oh, yes, indeed, she was in deep trouble.

"You?"

"What?" Try as she would, Bri couldn't control the slight tremor in her voice.

"I asked if you were hungry. Are you?"

"Yes." There was no way in hell she was going to run her gaze over him, no matter how much she wanted to do so. "And, as you said, we may as well eat now. I have menus." She handed one to him.

"Thanks." He smiled.

Damn him. Keeping the thought firmly inside her mind, where it belonged, she opened the menu and pretended to peruse the lunch specials even though she had already made her selection.

They didn't talk much or tarry during the meal, and within forty-five minutes of Bri having entered the café, they were back in the SUV and on the road.

Bri contained her patience until they were at last heading for the mountains.

"So what did you learn from your informant?" she asked when he remained silent.

He slanted a grin at her. "I thought you'd never ask. You surprised me by holding out for as long as you have."

"You have no idea how long I can hold out," she shot back at him, leaving it up to him to decide whether her response contained a double meaning.

He slanted a sideways, contemplative look at her, his eyes alight with devilment. "Is that a challenge?"

Bri raised her eyes and fluttered her eyelashes, her expression one of pure innocence. "Why, Mr. Wolfe," she said, her voice as close to a purr as she could make it, "a woman would have to be very brave to challenge you."

He gave a short bark of laughter. "Yeah, that's what I meant."

"You think I'm a brave woman?" Bri felt inordinately flattered even though she knew she was a brave woman. Her father had tested her, and she had passed his test of bravery and endurance. She had aced it, actually.

"Oh, yeah, you're brave," he said, sparing another glance at her. "You're brave and a bit reckless and, I'm afraid, very, very dangerous."

That last stopped her cold. She stared at him in astonishment. Her...dangerous? In what way? She had never deliberately harmed or intimidated anyone in her entire life.

"Dangerous to whom?" she asked, too bewildered by his remark to feel anything but puzzled.

Tanner sliced a smile at her that made her tingle all over. "I'd say you're dangerous to every male between the ages of fifteen and a hundred and fifteen."

Bri just couldn't hold back; she laughed.

"You don't think so, huh?"

"Of course I do," she said as her laughter subsided. "I'm sure every male out there between those ages is just trembling in fear of running into me. Get real, Wolfe," she said drolly. "I'm far from being dangerous to anyone of any age."

He slowed down a bit to give her a dry look. "Does that include the man we're on the hunt for?"

Bri stiffened. "That's different."

"In what way?"

"In the obvious way," she retorted, getting really rattled. "He's different. He's a killer."

"Yeah, he's a killer and a rapist," he agreed in an annoyingly reasonable tone. "But there are a lot of killers and rapists out there, and you're not on the hunt, packing heat, for them."

"No, I'm not," she snapped, getting seriously angry. "And that's because I'm not a hunter or a killer. But if we catch up to this…this monster, I will not hesitate a moment to use my weapon."

"Wait a minute." In an instant, Tanner practically stood on the brake, bringing the vehicle to a squealing, jarring stop. "You, me, neither one of us is going to shoot to kill him. Is that understood?"

He didn't wait for a response. "I'm warning you, Brianna, if you don't give me your word on this, I'll turn around, drive back to Durango and drop you at the Strater like you were on fire. I have never killed a man in my life and I'm not about to start now, and neither are you—not as long as you're with me. Have you got that?"

Bri didn't know whether to laugh or weep. She did neither; instead she calmly faced him. "I never so much as entertained the idea of killing the man, Tanner. I only meant I'd use my weapon to wing him, enough to bring him down. I don't want him dead. That's too easy."

He frowned. "Then what do you want?"

She hoped Tanner could actually see the icy determination on her tight lips. "I want to see him rot in prison for the rest of his life, living with his conscience—if he has one—and the memory of every woman he killed or hurt. I hope he lives to be one hundred and every day is spent in fear some other convict will decide to mete out his own brand of punishment."

Four

Tanner suppressed a shudder at the deadly, frigid tone of Brianna's voice, her cold expression. Wow, he thought, when this woman hates, she puts every part of herself into the lethal emotion. On the spot, he found himself hoping she never decided to turn that emotion on him.

"You still haven't told me what you learned from your informant."

The change in her was startling. Her tone had thawed to conversational, her expression, while not exactly warm, had relaxed somewhat. Swallowing a sigh of relief, Tanner put the SUV into gear and drove forward once more.

"He was seen leaving town two days ago. Apparently he's heading deep into the wildest section of the mountains. He left on horseback, leading a packhorse, and from the direction he was going, I suspect he's making his way to the Weminuche Wilderness."

Brianna frowned. "I vaguely recall having heard of it, but where and what is the Weminuche Wilderness?"

"The Weminuche is one of the largest designated wilderness areas in the country at somewhere around nine and a half thousand acres," he said, keeping his eyes on the inclining road. "While many tourists hike and bike in it, there are sections that are nearly inaccessible. It seems our man is heading in that direction."

"Well, if he is on horseback, leading a packhorse, I would think we could catch up to him in this SUV before he can reach one of those sections. Couldn't we?" She sounded satisfied with her deduction.

Tanner hated having to burst her confidence bubble, yet he had no choice. "No, we can't, Brianna. Even this vehicle can only go so far into the mountains. Later this afternoon, we'll stop for the night and go on by horseback in the morning."

She shot him a puzzled look. "But… How…I mean, where are we going to get horses out here?"

"I have a friend who owns a horse ranch tucked out of the way in a small valley." He shot her a grin before she had a chance to question him further. "We can spend tonight there."

By the quick glance he sent her, Tanner could tell by her expression she had questions, lots of questions, likely tripping over one another to see which one she could get out first. Within moments, she appeared to have sorted them out. She shot them out rapid-fire.

"How do you know your friend is there? How can you know we'll be welcome to spend the night? How can you be sure he'll have horses for hire? How—?" That's as far as he let her go.

"I know," he cut in, "because I know my friend. If he's not there when we arrive, he'll be out in the hills somewhere, and we'll wait until he returns."

"But—"

Tanner didn't hesitate to cut her off again. "Brianna, you'll have to trust me on this. We can't follow our man in this SUV. It can go a lot of places but not into the roughest terrain in the mountains."

"I understand that," she shot back impatiently. "But you just sprang this other person at me out of the blue. Who is he, other than your friend?"

"His name is Hawk," he began. Apparently she thought it was her turn to interrupt.

"What's his real name?"

"Hawk." He slanted a droll look at her. "His last name is McKenna. And, yes, he's a half-breed."

"I do not like that expression," Brianna said in a clipped, stern-teacher tone.

Tanner was hard put not to laugh. "Neither do I, but that's how Hawk refers to himself. He's not ashamed of his heritage. Matter of fact, he's proud to have both Scot and Apache blood in his veins." Now he laughed aloud, softly, almost as if to himself. "I think you'll find that Hawk is something else."

"And what might that something be?"

"Different," he said after a moment's silence. "He's one of a kind."

"One of a kind of what?" Her tone was clear warning she was getting edgy again.

Tanner shrugged. "One of a kind of man, of human being. I don't know how to explain it, he just is."

"Does he live alone?"

"Usually."

"Tanner…" There was a sharp note of impatience in her voice.

He laughed. "It's the truth, Brianna. Hawk is usually alone, but now and again he has his sister staying with him. Cat isn't as proud of her heritage."

She frowned. "Cat? Hawk and Cat?"

Tanner slid a quick grin at her. "Hawk is just that—Hawk. He's named after his maternal great-grandfather. Cat is short for Catriona, the Scot and Irish name for Catherine. She's named after her paternal great-great-grandmother."

"And she doesn't like being of mixed racial parentage," Brianna said, obviously choosing her words with care.

"No, she doesn't. So every so often she runs away from the world by hiding out with Hawk."

"Hiding out?" she nearly yelped. "Is he hiding out from the law?"

"No, Brianna, Hawk is not hiding from the law. He's not a criminal."

"Well, what is he, then? A hermit? Has he always lived away from society? How old is he?" She once again zapped the questions at him rapid-fire.

He shot the answers back at her in kind. "A man. No. Since he became an adult. I'm not sure—somewhere in his midthirties, I suppose."

"Odd," she murmured.

"Why?"

"Don't you think it's odd, a man deciding to live away from family, friends…women…at such a young age?"

Tanner shifted another glance at her. "I didn't say he was a cloistered monk, Brianna. When he's in the mood for company, he does see his family, friends." He paused deliberately, as she had. "And he does see women."

"You know—"

The SUV plowed over a natural speed bump, silencing her except for a startled, "Oh!"

"Sorry," he said, biting back laughter. "I told you it was rough—and it's going to get rougher." He couldn't hold back a slight grin. "A whole lot rougher."

She glanced around at the terrain, the narrow shoulders bordering the macadam road, and the thickening forest beyond. She frowned and shifted in her seat. "You said we'd stop at sunset. The sun's starting to track west now." She glanced around again. "Tanner…"

"There's a clearing up ahead," he said, anticipating her question as well as the need causing her suddenly restless shifting. He swept a hand in an encompassing movement. "We're in a national park area. Not only is there a clearing, there are restroom facilities."

Brianna sighed in relief. "I'm glad to hear it." She smiled. "I wasn't thrilled with the idea of asking you to stop while I made a dash into the bushes."

He laughed. "I know what you mean. I'm experiencing the, er, same pressure."

"Don't you dare make me laugh, Tanner Wolfe," she said. "I would rather not embarrass myself, thank you."

"Well, you're in luck, Brianna Stewart," he assured her. "The clearing is just beyond the bend up ahead."

"Here we are," he said moments later, pulling the vehicle into a spacious clearing by the side of the road. Along one side of the area, just beyond a posted sign reading Restrooms, was a good-size building. They headed toward it quickly.

Within minutes, they were back on the road. An hour and a half later, Tanner made a quick turn.

"What exactly— Oh!" she said, startled by the jostling of the SUV as he drove off the paved road onto a dirt, stone-strewn track undeserving of the name *road*. "Where are you going?" Bri demanded, glancing at the forest, which seemed to be closing in on them.

"To Hawk's place." He shot a flashing glance at her frown. "What? You expected Hawk to be living smack-dab in the middle of a superhighway?"

Bri's frown turned into a scowl. "No, of course not," she said, one hand gripping the edge of the seat, the other clinging to the dash in an attempt to keep from being flung back and forth within the confines of the seat belt like a rag doll.

"Just hang on," Tanner said, his grip solid on the steering wheel. "It's gonna get worse before it gets better."

"I…d-didn't…think it c-could get any worse," she finished in a rush.

"Ah, honey, you're in for a bouncy surprise."

She sighed, ignored the cramping in her fingers and glared at him. "I told you not to call me 'honey.'"

Tanner laughed all the way down the track to the valley that spread away from it at the bottom. Tucked on the leeward side of the mountain was a one-story ranch house much like the ones seen in Western movies.

Hawk's place was hardly the small, run-down outfit Bri had been expecting to find. In the waning afternoon light she could see several rail-fenced corrals, all containing horses, their coats gleaming in the slanted sunlight. But the ranch was the least of the surprises in store for her.

Bri was so distracted by looking around the property she never noticed Hawk McKenna standing in the shadows of the wraparound porch until he stepped out into the light. At his side stood the biggest dog she had ever seen. More like a pony.

Her startled gaze watched man and animal as they sauntered toward the vehicle Tanner pulled to a stop.

Hawk was not quite as tall as Tanner, but slimmer, rangier. Though older, McKenna was every bit as handsome as Tanner, if in a different, somewhat rougher way.

Where the younger man's appearance was sculpted, Hawk's features had a harshly rough-hewn look. His hair was even longer but as clean and well kept as Tanner's. Most startling of all, it was the same shade of brown and, in the golden glow of slanting sun rays, shot with streaks as dark-red as Bri's own.

Tanner got out of the truck and the two men hugged like long-lost brothers. The dog, not barking or whining, just stood beside his master as if waiting for his turn to greet the company.

As soon as the men were done hugging and slapping each other on the back, the animal moved to Tanner. When he greeted the dog, it jumped up, front paws on his shoulders, standing almost as tall as Tanner.

"Hey, Boyo. No kisses, not on my face," Tanner

said, laughing as he twisted his head to avoid the excited dog's eager reception. "Yeah, the hand's okay." Still laughing, he ruffled the dog's coat.

Boyo, Bri thought. What kind of name was that for such a large dog? He was massive, formidable, his silvery-gray coat marked by small streaks of black. Fortunately the dog appeared friendly or she wouldn't have considered stepping foot from the safety of the SUV.

Tanner's sudden appearance at her door broke into her concentration on the animal.

"Brianna, are you getting out?" He grinned, pulled her door open. "Or are your fingers locked on the seat and dash?"

Startled from her inspection of the dog, Bri gave him a dry look and a blatant lie. "I'm afraid to move, since I feel as if every bone in my body was disjointed during the ride down here."

"I thought maybe you were terrified by the sight of Boyo."

"That, too," she admitted. "But I see he's friendly." She frowned. "What kind of name is Boyo for an animal his size?"

"It's Irish for *boy*," he explained, laughing again. "Come on, Hawk will protect you."

Lord, Bri loved the sound of his laughter. Steeling herself against her feelings, she took the hand he held out to her.

His hand wasn't soft, his nails weren't mani-cured as were the hands of her father and most of the other men she knew. His broad, long fingers were used to work, hardened and rough.

An image flashed before her with sudden clarity. His rough hands caressing her body, gripping her bottom to draw him closer as he crushed his mouth to hers.

A tremor shot through her.

"Are you cold, Brianna?" Tanner frowned, placing the other hand at her waist to steady her as she jumped to the ground.

"No…" Bri took a quick breath, stalling for time to come up with a reasonable excuse. "I'm hungry." Was that reasonable enough? "It's been a long time since lunch, don't forget. Aren't you hungry?" She stretched and took a few steps, easing the stiffness in her back from sitting so long and being jarred on the drive into the valley.

"Plenty to eat in the house," Hawk said.

"Come on, Bri. Come meet Hawk." Tanner gently took her by the arm to lead her around the SUV toward his friend. "And Boyo."

Hawk McKenna had a solid handshake and a winning smile. For some inexplicable reason, she instantly both liked and trusted him. Something inside told her this was a good man. Something about him reminded her of Tanner.

Wait a minute. Tanner…good? Trustworthy? She had to admit her mental jury was still out on that verdict.

Boyo stood by his master, his long, black-tipped

tail swishing back and forth, his body trembling in eagerness to greet her.

Bri tentatively reached out a hand to the animal to sniff.

"You may touch him," Hawk said, his deep voice edged with amusement. "He won't bite you."

She touched the dog's muzzle and was promptly rewarded by a swipe of his tongue. Laughing, Bri caressed his head, scratched him under his wide jaw and ran her hand over his back. The rough, wiry feel of his coat against her palm surprised her; he had looked so sleek and smooth.

"You have a nice spread here, Mr. McKenna," she said, glancing up at him, her compliment sincere.

"Thank you." He smiled at her before sweeping the property with an appreciative look. "It's home."

He led them to the house, Boyo in step on the far side of him.

"Welcome," Hawk said as he pushed the door open, stepping back and sweeping his arm in invitation.

Boyo trotted into the kitchen, and within moments they could hear him lapping up water.

"Thank you." Bri smiled at him as she stepped into what was obviously the living room. She glanced around her at the sparse yet homey decor.

"This is very nice," she said, turning to smile at Hawk. "Navajo?" she asked, indicating a beautifully woven blanket hanging on one wall.

"Yeah," Hawk answered. "A gift from a friend."

"It's lovely." Bri smiled, moving forward for a closer look. "You have nice friends. That blanket must be worth a small fortune."

"It is. And I do." Hawk nodded and glanced at Tanner. "And Wolfe, there, is the friend." He smiled, slow and easy. "Wanna tell Ms. Stewart what you paid for the blanket, Tanner?"

"No." Tanner shook his head but smiled back. "He earned it, Brianna," he explained. "He helped me track a man, a real badass, two years ago. The jerk was a multiple killer with a big bounty on his head." He shot a dry look at Hawk. "I wanted to share the bounty with him. He said no but that he'd accept a particular blanket. You see—"

"Wolfe," Hawk said, a warning in his tone.

"You don't scare me, ole son, so save your breath." Tanner grinned at him.

Hawk narrowed his eyes. Tanner's grin widened.

Fearing that any second they'd be at each other, fists flying, Bri held a hand in the air in the signal to halt. "Don't start anything here, you two. This house is too beautiful to wreck it in a free-for-all." Her voice was soft but stern. "If you're going to beat up on each other, take it outside."

Tanner and Hawk stared at each other a moment, then roared with laughter.

Bri placed her hands on her hips, glared at the two of them and tapped one booted foot on the hardwood floor. "I do hope you're not laughing at me." Though pleasant, her voice held a sting.

"Wouldn't dream of it, ma'am." Hawk was obviously fighting to contain a grin.

"Never gave it a thought, *ma'am*." Tanner didn't bother to hold back a grin. He laughed out loud.

"O-kay. I've had enough of your silliness." Bri was having difficulty maintaining the laughter rising in her throat. "I need a bathroom first, a proper bath and something to eat. Oh, and my pack."

Hawk slanted a sober look at Tanner. "She always this bossy?"

Tanner nodded, sighing. "'Fraid so. It's enough to drive a simple man to distraction."

Bri rolled her eyes and opened her mouth to blast the two of them. She wasn't fast enough.

"Yeah." Tanner gave a slow head shake. "I just don't know what to do with her."

Bri was torn between amusement and annoyance. She was silent just long enough for Hawk to get in another shot.

"Oh, buddy, I'd know what to do with her." Teasing laughter danced in his dark eyes.

"Well, yeah, but—"

That's as far as she let Tanner get. "But you're going to be too busy getting my gear from the SUV. Right?" Her tone held a definite warning.

"Er, yeah, right, I'm on it." Softly chuckling, Tanner turned and strode out the door.

"And I'm gonna finish supper." Hawk headed for the kitchen, clearly visible in the open floor plan, flicking a hand toward a hallway on the far side of the living room. "Bathroom's the second door to the left."

"Thank you." Bri headed for the hallway, hearing Hawk ask Boyo if he was hungry, too.

She was washing her hands, grimacing at her appearance in the mirror, when a soft knock sounded on the door.

"I've brought your pack, Brianna. Should I leave it here, outside the door?"

"No." She opened said door as he finished speaking. "I'll take it. Thank you." She rewarded him with her most brilliant smile, took the pack and then closed the door in his face.

"Whoa," Tanner murmured on an exhaled breath, thinking Brianna had the most beautiful and arousing smile he had ever had aimed at him. His jeans were suddenly tight, chafing him in a delicate part of his body.

The sound of the shower reached him through the door. Tanner imagined her standing under the tingling spray, naked and wet, the water sluicing down her slim body. Not only did his jeans get tighter, his chest grew tight, too.

Damn, get away from the door, Wolfe, before you explode and embarrass yourself by having to listen to McKenna laugh his ass off.

Drawing deep breaths and telling himself he could control his own body, his automatic reactions to a beautiful woman, Tanner gathered up the gear at his feet and headed to the bedrooms. He opened the door just enough to place Brianna's gear inside the room Hawk had designated as hers, the one Cat stayed in when she visited. From there he went to his room, the one he always used when he stayed at Hawk's place.

By the time Tanner nonchalantly strolled into the kitchen, he, aided by a cold shower, had worked his mind over matter...at least enough that it didn't show.

"Your lady friend is something, Wolfe," Hawk said, leveling a hard look at Tanner. "But why in hell did you bring her along on a hunt?"

"I didn't have a choice," he began, but apparently Hawk wasn't hearing him.

"Are you trying to get that beautiful creature killed?" Hawk demanded.

Tanner sighed. "I told you, I didn't have a—"

"Choice," Brianna finished for him in a decisive tone. "I played the trump card."

"Yeah," Tanner muttered, turning to look at her. Brianna stood in the entrance to the kitchen area, her still-wet hair hanging straight down her back, her face free of makeup, but glowing from her shower.

"What trump card?" Hawk frowned, glancing between his two guests, who continued to stare at each other.

"Money," they answered in unison.

Hawk arched his dark brows. "I like money," he

said, his voice laconic. "Though not enough to endanger a beautiful woman—or any woman, for that matter—by taking her along on a manhunt for a killer." His gaze narrowed on Tanner. "How much money are we talking about?"

Tanner switched his steely stare to Hawk. "An impressive amount of money."

Hawk smiled—well, almost—and turned his narrowed gaze on Brianna. "How much?" It wasn't a question so much as an order.

"A million dollars."

Tanner admired her cool composure. Not many people, men or women, could withstand that particular piercing look from Hawk. In the next few minutes, Brianna ratcheted up his admiration for her even further.

Hawk whistled. "That's a lot of dollars."

Flashing her traffic-stopping smile, she nodded in agreement. "Yes, it is." The smile fled, replaced by a haughty expression. "I take it you disapprove."

"I don't disapprove of the money," Hawk said with a quick shake of his head. "But I do disapprove of Tanner taking along a woman."

"Yet there are women bounty hunters," she retorted. "Are there not?"

"She used that same argument on me," Tanner inserted, just to remind them he was still there.

Hawk flicked a look at him.

Brianna ignored him.

"I don't approve of women bounty hunters, either. It's too dangerous for a woman."

"Indeed." Brianna's voice was icy.

"Yeah, indeed." Hawk matched her tone.

Tanner grinned, not that either one of them noticed. They were too busy trying to stare each other down. This should be interesting, he mused, settling down in a kitchen chair to watch the battle of wills.

No one knew better than he that Hawk was nothing if not tenacious. On the other hand, Tanner had personal knowledge of how stubborn Brianna could be. Yes, indeedy, he thought, controlling an urge to laugh, this should prove very interesting.

Brianna sighed as if sorely tried. "As I pointed out to your friend, I have had excellent training. I am well equipped to take care of myself."

With that, she had lobbed the ball into Hawk's court. Tanner waited for the return volley.

Hawk slammed it back at her. "I don't give a f—" He caught himself up short before finishing with, "freaking damn how well you've been trained. You don't belong in the mountains, tracking a criminal."

Whoa. Tanner stared at his friend in surprise. Hawk was losing his cool, and that didn't happen often. Tanner decided it was time to referee this match.

"Okay, boys and girls," he said, pushing himself from the chair to step between the two combatants. "Take a break. It's time for a truce."

"But, dammit, Tanner, it's just not safe!"

"Save your breath, ole buddy," Tanner said,

shaking his head. "I went through all that with her, chapter and verse." He shot a quick glance at her face, her expression one of detachment. "It's like talking to a brick wall."

"How charming, so complimentary," Brianna coolly inserted. "But can we drop the subject now? I'm so hungry I could eat a.. brick wall, maybe." A smile teased her lips and danced in her bright eyes.

"Told you so," Tanner said with a grin, chiding Hawk.

Hawk heaved a deep sigh. "I give up."

"Good." She rewarded him with a charming smile. Too soon.

"On one condition," Hawk went on, challenge hard on his voice.

Bri narrowed her eyes. "What condition?"

Tanner frowned, wondering what Hawk was up to now.

"You take Boyo with you."

"But…" she began in protest.

"Good idea, Hawk," Tanner said, deciding it was time to end this match. "Brianna, Boyo is a good hunter. You know, the Irish wolfhounds were bred to hunt and bring down wolves and elk."

"Wolves?" She shifted her gaze to the dog, who had cocked his head at the sound of his name. "Well, he certainly looks big enough and strong enough for it. But he doesn't seem natured to do that. He's as friendly as a puppy."

"Of course he is," Hawk agreed. "Here he's a big, sloppy sweetheart. Matter of fact, most wolf-hounds are simply house pets these days. But take him out hunting, turn him loose on a scent, and he reverts to breed and can be one mean son of a—" Again, he caught himself from cursing. "He can be rough."

"But..." she began.

Tanner smothered laughter to interrupt her. "You may as well give in, Brianna. Hawk can be as stubborn as you, maybe even more so."

"Oh, all right. We'll take Boyo...but only if I get food—pronto."

Hawk slid a look at Brianna, a smile twitching the corners of his mouth. "Man, you're tough. But you win. Food's ready. Let's eat."

Tanner lost it and let loose the laughter he had been holding back.

Hawk followed in kind.

Brianna looked from one to the other before her laughter blended with theirs. She was first to regain control. "Okay, you clowns, what's for supper?" She gave a dainty sniff. "Whatever it is, it smells wonderful."

Hawk sobered except for a lingering chuckle. "It's chili. Hope you like it spicy."

"Love it," she said.

Tanner wasn't surprised. He'd figured Brianna Stewart wouldn't have it any other way.

Five

Bri sighed with contentment as she dabbed her lips with a napkin. The chili was delicious. And spicy. She had hungrily finished off two bowlfuls, along with several slices of Hawk's homemade corn bread.

"That was a wonderful meal," she said to her host. "Thank you."

"You're welcome." Apparently pleased with her response, Hawk pushed back his chair and stood. "Are you ready for coffee and dessert now?" He glanced from Bri to Tanner.

"Coffee," Bri answered without hesitation. "But I couldn't eat another bite."

"Just coffee for me, too," Tanner said.

When they had finished their coffee, Bri stood up and began clearing the table.

"You don't have to help," Hawk said.

"I know. But I want to do it." She shooed him away with a hand. "You two go relax or something."

"You win. I don't often get out of kitchen duty." Hawk led the way outside to let Tanner choose the horses for the hunt.

At the door, Tanner paused to tell Bri how to find the room where he had stashed her gear. No sooner had he shut the door behind him when Hawk lit into him.

"Are you out of your mind?" he demanded, striding for the stables.

Tanner sighed. "Don't start, McKenna. I had my fill arguing with Brianna back in Durango. I'm not in the mood to argue with you."

Hawk snorted. "In the mood or not, you're getting an argument. Dammit, Wolfe—"

That's as far as he got before Tanner cut him off. "Yeah, dammit. Hell, double dammit. What else was I supposed to do?"

Reaching the stable, Hawk yanked the door open and flicked on the lights to illuminate the dim interior. "How about making it clear you wouldn't bring her. End of argument. Period."

"I tried that." Tanner gave his best friend a fierce scowl. "Didn't work. She told me if I refused, I should forget it, she'd find herself another hunter." He exhaled in a bid to ease the tension riding him.

"And you didn't want to give up a big payoff?"

"Are you nuts?" Now Tanner was getting angry. "Hawk, you know me better than that. And you know as well as I do there are bounty hunters out there that will agree to any conditions, even to allowing a woman to hunt with them, if the price is right."

Now Hawk sighed. "I know. But I don't like this at all. Brianna is a beautiful woman. A nice woman." He strode inside. "I'd hate like hell to see her hurt."

"Don't feel like the Lone Ranger. I feel the same way." His mouth curved into a wry smile. "That's why I'm not taking her along."

Hawk narrowed his eyes suspiciously. "Aah, are you saying what I think you're saying?"

"You got it, ole buddy." He grinned. "I'm leaving her here, in your capable hands."

"But what the hell's the difference if you leave her in Durango or here with me?"

"Hawk, you're not thinking," Tanner chided him. "If I'd have left her in Durango, she'd have either contacted another hunter or set out on her own." He shuddered. "I don't even want to think about that. Out here, with you, she's stuck. All she can do is ask you to drive her back to Durango."

"Where she will promptly look up and hire another hunter," Hawk pointed out.

"I know, but by then I'll be way ahead of the pack, so to speak."

Hawk shook his head as if in frustration. "And when you bring him in and hand him over to the law, you know damn well she will likely hand you a check for the original ten grand posted."

"I know." Tanner nodded. "And I don't care. Hawk, it's no longer the money. It's Brianna and her safety." He paused before continuing. "I'm attracted to her. Very attracted. It was there from the minute I opened my door and saw her standing there."

A small smile tugged at Hawk's lips. "That's understandable. Brianna's gorgeous and sexy as hell."

"Tell me about it." Tanner shook his head. "She had no sooner walked into my place and I wanted to swing her up into my arms and…well, never mind. I'm sure you can figure it out for yourself."

"Sure." Hawk nodded. "I've been there."

"I have, too, but not like this," Tanner admitted. "This is stronger than—" He broke off. "The point is, I couldn't leave her in Durango and I can't take her with me. This Minnich creep is a killer. He's killed at least one woman, and the law suspects there's more. If anything happened to her, if he got a chance to harm her in any way, I swear I'd go berserk." He shuddered at the very idea of Brianna injured. "Hawk, I can't take her with me. I can't take that chance."

Hawk nodded. "There's the hunter I know and love like a brother. You had me a tad worried that you had slipped a cog."

Tanner laughed. "Not to worry. Now let's look at horses."

Hawk paused at the second stall inside the stable. "We're going to have to play it cool, you know?"

"Yeah." Tanner nodded. "We can't take a chance of her getting suspicious. Leave the lights on in here when we leave. I'll bring her out to show her the horses we've chosen."

"Show her the mare." Hawk indicated the chocolate-brown horse in the third stall. "She would be the logical choice for a woman."

In no time, Brianna had the kitchen spotless and went in search of her room, musing on the idea that Boyo obviously liked her, for he padded after her.

Finding the room easily, Bri stepped inside, and immediately wondered if Hawk had frequent visits from lady friends. The bedroom had definite feminine touches, including a vanity table and bench, the surface littered with an array of skin-care products, makeup and a silver-backed comb-and-brush set.

Along the back wall was a queen-size bed, set between two windows through which the last rays of sunlight shone. Crossing the room, Bri drew back a sheer curtain panel to stare out at the vista. A huge meadow spread out from the side of the house and along the foothills of the mountain. She was puzzled for a moment by a large, flat, whitish circle on the ground a good distance from the house.

Then realization dawned. The white circle was a helicopter pad, right there on the edge of the meadow.

How convenient, she thought, smiling as she turned away from the window. A chopper would come in very handy when snow blocked the roadways in the dead of winter.

She had to smile. Boyo had made himself comfortable and lay stretched out on the foot of the bed as if it were his right to do so. Deciding it probably was, she walked back across the room, sitting down at the vanity to gaze into the mirror. Her hair, drying now, twirled into its natural waves. Her face appeared pale and dull. Bri was considering whether to retrieve her makeup case when she heard the front door open, close again and Tanner call to her.

"Brianna, Hawk's making a fresh pot of coffee. Do you want some?"

Sliding off the bench, she went to the door and called back, "Yes, I'll be right there." Glancing at the dog, she said, "You coming?" Boyo lifted his large head to give her a soulful look, then his head plopped back onto the mattress.

Guess not. A soft smile on her lips, she glanced again in the mirror, shrugged and left the room, thinking the hell with the hair and makeup. If Tanner and Hawk didn't like her bare face and unruly waves, they could just get over it.

"I like your hair down like that," Tanner said as she strolled into the kitchen. He grinned. "All kinda wild and loose around your face."

Bri gave him a droll look. "Thank you." Might

as well admit to the truth, she thought, smiling back at him. "I didn't bother to brush it."

"You didn't need to bother," Hawk said, placing two steaming mugs on the table. Crossing to the countertop to retrieve the third, he tossed over his shoulder, "You're among friends."

"I would hope so, as it's two to one here." She calmly glanced from Hawk to Tanner. "Not that those are bad odds, you understand, or that I couldn't handle the two of you. But it could get ugly."

Silence for a moment. Then both men broke up with laughter.

"I like this gal's style, Wolfe," Hawk said between lingering chuckles. "She might even be able to handle you, maverick that you are."

"I wouldn't bet the ranch on it, ole buddy," Tanner advised in a slow drawl.

Could she handle him? Bri asked herself hours later as she lay in the wide bed, staring at the diffuse moonlight shimmering on the ceiling through the sheer curtains. That same question had played games with her mind throughout the rest of the evening.

As soon as they had finished their coffee, Tanner had taken her to the stables to show her the horses Hawk had chosen for their use. Tanner's mount was a big roan with a shiny dark-red coat. For Brianna he had picked a brown mare, smaller than the roan but with a sweet temperament. The minute Brianna stretched out her palm, the mare poked her head over the gate on the stall.

Pleased with Hawk's selections, Bri introduced herself to the horses, talking softly to each as she stroked their noses and long necks in turn.

"I noticed from the bedroom window that Hawk has a helipad in the back pasture," she said later as they walked back to the house. "Does he own and fly his own personal helicopter?"

"No. He has the pad because he's alone out here most of the time. Although Hawk is a careful man by nature, accidents can always happen—to humans and animals. He installed the pad for convenience and for a quicker medical rescue response if needed." He tossed her a grin. "But, though he has lived here for a long time, he put in the pad only after Cat began using the ranch for a vacation getaway when she needed some space to be herself, breathe fresh air, roam free on the grounds."

"I see," Bri said, but then shook her head. "No, I guess I don't see. I can understand her wanting to visit her brother, but you said before she uses Hawk's place for a hideout. From what?"

"From the city, the crowds, the polluted air. Also from the jerks who get their kicks by making cracks about her heritage."

Anger flashed through her like a bolt of lightning. "I detest that sort of thing."

"Hey, don't attack me," Tanner said in a calming tone. "I feel the same way. But, like it or not, I'm afraid there are still some Neanderthals screwing up society. Men like the animal who attacked your sister and raped and killed her friend."

"I know." Bri nodded, exhaling to release the anger. "I have to deal with the crude type occasionally in the library."

"You work in a library?"

"Yes. I'm a research librarian at the University of Pennsylvania."

"The men come on to you, make suggestive remarks?" His voice carried an edgy note.

Confused by the sudden sharpness of his tone, she gave him a quick glance. His expression was bland, but his eyes were cold. Now what was biting him?

"Well?" he prompted, his voice now as cold as his eyes. "What did the crude jerks say to you?"

"Oh, the usual." She shrugged. "You know, juvenile things like, 'Oh, I've found the ice-queen types are always the hottest.'"

"Wonderful." His lip curled. "How smooth. How very debonair." He shook his head. "That line should have all the women falling on their backs for him. Stupid kids."

Bri shot a droll look at him. "That particular line came from one of the professors."

Tanner stared at her a moment, then laughed. "Some men never grow up, do they, no matter how smart and well-educated they are."

"So it seems," Bri agreed with him, smiling as they strolled toward the house.

When they reached the porch, he came to a stop, turning to face her, grasping her shoulders. "I guess I'm no smarter than the others."

"What do you mean?" Her voice began to fade and her breathing grew erratic, strained, as he lowered his head to hers.

"Fool that I am," he murmured, his lips barely a half inch from hers, "I'm going to kiss you, Brianna."

"Yes...please..." Her voice was swallowed up inside his mouth.

Incredible. His mouth claiming hers was absolutely incredible. And exciting. His tongue slid inside, sweeping every nook, tangling with her own.

Bri curled her arms around his taut neck, moving her body closer to him, against him. His arms circled her waist, drawing her closer still. Something seemed to sizzle through every cell of her being as he ground into her, making her all too aware of his erection.

Good heavens! She had never been kissed like this. At the time she had believed Mr. Smooth and Charming had been good, but he was a novice compared to the man she was now clinging to as tightly as ivy clings to a brick wall.

She wanted to cry out in protest when he lifted his head. She swallowed to keep it inside. "That was some kiss," she said, striving for normal, attaining something similar to a croak.

"Yeah, it felt like more." Releasing her, he stepped back, shaking his head. "But I'm not that much of a fool...I hope."

Bri didn't know whether to feel insulted or flattered. She felt confused. Who wouldn't be when a man called himself a fool for kissing her? Numb, she allowed him to lead her into the house.

From then on he was all business—except for the occasional brush of his arm or his hand against her. Bri had reached a point in her life where she believed there were no accidents. She knew his touches were deliberate.

But why? That was the question nagging at her tired and befuddled mind. Nevertheless, she and Tanner went through their gear, deciding, along with the occasional suggestion from Hawk and nose nudge from Boyo, what they should take.

Bri was relieved to learn they were taking a pack animal, which allowed her to take a few items more than the absolute essentials. One of those items was a bag of dark chocolate Hershey's Kisses she had stashed in an inner pocket of her backpack.

"You can't have any," she murmured to the curious dog sniffing at the pack. She ruffled his wiry coat, lowering her head to whisper, "They can make you very sick, and that would make me very, very sad."

The gear packed and ready for an early departure, Bri had excused herself and gone to her room, Boyo at her side. Once in the room, the dog again stretched out on the foot of the bed. Yawning, Bri curled under the plump comforter, as the night had grown much cooler.

Though it had been a long day, she couldn't go to sleep. Her mind was restless, repeating the same thoughts over and over.

Could she handle Tanner Wolfe?

Did she want to?

Damned straight, she wanted to.

Tanner couldn't sleep. Even with his eyes squeezed shut, an image of Brianna shimmered before him, teasing his mind, tormenting his libido. That kiss, that blazing, scorching kiss. Would he ever get the memory of it out of his mind, his senses?

"Damn," he muttered, tossing aside the comforter to allow the chill night air to cool his overheated body. "Stop reacting like a damn fool nineteen-year-old kid," he grumbled, shifting position. "You've got a job to do. Get your mind off the woman and onto controlling your imagination and your hormones. There's a lot of money at stake here…if she even pays you more than the original ten thousand posted."

That last animal-like growl silenced him. Money?

He hadn't really given a thought to the money since explaining his situation to Hawk. When had the money become secondary? *Secondary?* Tanner's now-overactive mind repeated. Secondary to what?

"Brianna." He whispered her name like a prayer. Brianna. Her name echoed inside his head like a mantra. She was the most unlikely woman. A gun-toting librarian. A woman of privilege who knew how to shoot and ride and track. Not at all the type he normally consorted with, he reminded himself, let alone fell for.

Jesus. When had she become so important to him? Not simply her safety but her, the woman? The woman he wanted more than he had ever wanted any woman before.

In that instant he knew without a doubt he would spend the rest of his life hunting down that killer, if necessary. Not for the money, Tanner thought, deciding then and there not to accept any, but for Brianna, for her peace of mind.

He would do it even at the loss of his own peace of mind…not to mention his sanity.

Tanner knew Brianna would not be there when he returned to Durango. He knew, as well, that she would never want to see him again.

Still, he ached for her, ached to be with her in the most intimate way a man could be with a woman. Tanner pulled the comforter around his body, which was both shivering and burning for Brianna.

Damn. What was the matter with him?

Tanner snorted. As if he didn't know. Still, he wouldn't admit it, not even to himself.

Six

A light tap and a murmured "Brianna" woke Bri. Frowning, her eyes barely open, she wondered why Hawk and not Tanner had come to wake her.

"I'm awake," she muttered, raking her fingers through sleep-tangled hair. Other than a small night-light plugged into a wall socket, the room was dark, and she reached to the nightstand to switch on the light.

"Coffee's fresh and hot."

"Give me a couple of minutes." Yawning, she tossed the cover back, grinning as Boyo lifted his large head, alert and apparently ready for anything.

"Hi, fella," she said, ruffling his hair. "Go back to sleep, you don't have to get up yet."

Obviously Boyo wasn't about to do any such thing as go to sleep. After stretching his legs, he jumped from the bed and padded to the door, waiting patiently until Bri opened it for him.

The hallway was well lighted, as was the living room beyond. Smiling, she wondered if Hawk had turned on every light in the house. That is, until she opened the bathroom door.

The bright sunlight filling the room jolted her like a shock. What the heck time was it? she asked herself, frowning as she entered the room. Hadn't Tanner said he wanted to get an early start?

Puzzled, she nevertheless took a quick shower and ran back to the bedroom to look at the clock she hadn't bothered to glance at before. The digital numbers flashed 8:45. Stunned, she pulled the heavy blackout drapes over the sheers aside, staring in disbelief at the blaze of sunlight pouring through the window.

Suspicion tickling the back of her mind, Bri quickly dressed, braided her hair and left the room, following the aroma of fresh coffee.

Hawk stood by the stove. Boyo had his nose buried in his food bowl. There was no sign of Tanner or the gear he had set by the door last night.

The tickle of suspicion expanded into certainty. "Where's Tanner?" Her voice was cold, her stance stiff, her eyes narrowed.

"He's gone…left about five," he answered, warm compassion meeting her icy stare.

"Gone?" she repeated, voice rising an octave. "He left without me? That son of a—"

"Now, Brianna," Hawk cut her off in a soft, calming tone. "Come have a cup of coffee and some breakfast and I'll explain everything to you."

Annoyance curdled her tone. "Don't speak to me as if I were a child, Hawk."

"I'm not," he said, still soothingly calm. "I'm speaking to you as if you were an intelligent, mature adult. Now, please, come and sit down."

Still stiff with outrage at the deceiving rat Tanner, she nevertheless moved into the kitchen and sat down at the table. What else could she do? Rant and rave? She could do that sitting down over coffee.

Mere moments after her bottom hit the chair seat, Hawk set a plate of bacon, scrambled eggs and toast in front of her, followed by a steaming mug of coffee.

She sat there looking at the food, only sipping her coffee. She was way too angry to eat.

"I know you're angry," Hawk said, taking a seat across from her, "and I suppose you have every right to be. But not eating isn't going to solve a thing. Tell you what—you eat a little something, and I'll explain Tanner's reasons for leaving without you."

"I already know his so-called reasons. He doesn't want me, any woman or any*one* else hunting with him...the rat." Her voice dropped to a deeper, arrogant tone, mimicking Tanner's. "'Like it or not, I hunt alone.'"

"Yep, that's Tanner," Hawk agreed, surprising her. "Well, now that we agree on that, suppose you attack your breakfast."

Bri rolled her eyes. She drew a breath to tell him what to do with his breakfast, but in so doing got a whiff of the food, and her stomach growled. She gave in immediately.

To her surprise, Bri finished every morsel on her plate and every drop of coffee. Without being asked, Hawk refilled her mug.

"Thank you. Breakfast was delicious," she said, taking a careful sip of the hot brew. "Now I'm ready to hear Tanner's reasons for stranding me here."

Hawk smiled. "First of all, Brianna, you're not stranded. Second, he actually didn't deceive you."

Bri's back went ramrod stiff. "What do you mean? He deserted me when he said he would take me with him."

"And he did, in his way," Hawk countered. "He took you out of Durango and brought you here."

"That's not funny." She was getting steamed all over again. Suddenly her delicious breakfast lay heavy in her stomach. "He didn't say he'd bring me here, dammit! He said he'd take me along hunting with him."

Hawk was shaking his head. "He couldn't, Brianna."

"That's ridiculous." She glared at him. "He selected horses. Showed me the mare I was to ride. Stashed my gear next to his own by the door.

And now you tell me he couldn't take me. Why the hell not?"

Bri realized she was on the edge of losing it. She paused to breathe, calm herself down.

"He told me he could not—would not—expose you to the danger of possibly facing a killer."

"And I told him I can take care of myself, and Tanner knows it."

"I'm sure he does." Hawk nodded. "But then, I'm also sure it makes no difference to him." He gave her a gentle look. "Although I know Tanner's feelings about hunting alone, there is more to it in this instance."

"What?" Bri frowned. "What other reason, other than his pure, arrogant bullheadedness?"

Hawk sighed. "Your safety is important to him, Brianna. Very important."

Bri felt a tiny flare deep inside. Could Hawk possibly mean that Tanner cared for her? Oh, she was aware of the physical attraction between them. All too aware. But could he feel something stronger than that?

The mere idea, the thought alone, caused excitement to dance along her nerve endings. Then she came to her senses, telling herself to grow up and face reality. Tanner didn't care for her. He treated her the way he would any woman who wanted to hunt a killer.

But it was a lovely thought…for a moment.

Sighing softly, she lowered her head so Hawk

couldn't see the disappointment mirrored in her eyes.

"Okay," he said, sliding his chair back and standing. "I'll get these dishes cleared away and then I'll drive you back to Durango."

Bri snapped her head up. "I'm not going back to Durango," she said with quiet determination.

"You want to wait here for Tanner to return?" He hurried on before she could reply. "Not that I mind, you understand, but—"

"No, Hawk, I'm going after him."

"Alone?" Hawk stared at her. "Brianna, you should know it's never smart or safe to hunt alone." He shook his head. "This man is a killer."

Bri blinked, shook her head. "No, no, I'm not going after Minnich. I'm going after Tanner."

"It's just as dangerous."

"I'll be careful," she assured him.

"What if you get lost?"

Bri gave him a long look. "I do know how to blaze a trail, Hawk."

"But—"

"No buts," she said, shaking her head again. "I am going. Will you give me the use of a horse? I'll pay you the going rate."

"No." Flat, final.

Nothing could have made her reveal the hurt his refusal gave her. "Okay, I'll trek." She moved to rise, but Hawk held up a hand.

"You don't understand. I meant I won't accept

payment for the horse," he explained. "You can take any one you like."

Bri blinked against a rush of grateful tears. "Thank you, Hawk."

"You'll also need a pack animal."

"No, thank you. Another animal would slow me down. I want to catch up with Tanner before he catches up to Minnich." She started to leave the kitchen, but Hawk stopped her.

"Brianna, you'll need supplies and food. You can't go tracking Tanner without them."

"I've got trail mix and beef jerky in my pack." This time she did smile, keeping the chocolate to herself. "My father taught me early on to always carry some with me, just in case."

"You'll need more than that." He sighed. "I'll pack some food and water into saddlebags as soon as I finish up here." He raised his eyebrows. "Do you have all your stuff together?"

"All but the last-minute things," she said, once again heading out of the kitchen. "It'll take only a few minutes to get them."

Fully aware of the passing of time—time in which Tanner got farther away from the ranch—Bri quickly gathered her toiletries. Then she made up the bed and strode back down the hall.

Hawk wasn't there. For a moment Bri stood still, afraid she had been abandoned again. But common sense prevailed. Boyo sat by her backpack, glancing from the door to her and back to the door, obviously waiting for his master to return. She waited with him.

A few minutes later, Hawk walked back inside. "I saddled the mare Tanner showed you last night. Okay?"

"Yes." She smiled. "She's a sweetie."

"I'll get the saddlebags ready." He went into the kitchen.

Bri knelt down to say goodbye to the dog. "You're a sweetie, too," she murmured.

"I want you to take the sweetie with you," Hawk said, helping her to rise. "And no arguments," he went on as she opened her mouth to do just that. "As I said last night, he'll protect you to the death. And I've given him Tanner's scent." He smiled. "Boyo will find him, and you won't need to blaze a trail. In case he doesn't find him, he'll find his way home."

Circling her arms around Hawk, Bri gave him a big hug. "Thanks for everything," she said, stepping back to smile up at him.

Hawk's high-boned cheeks wore a flush of pleasure and embarrassment. "No—thank you, Brianna. You're one to ride the river with."

Aware of the old Western saying, complimenting her grit and suitability, Bri grinned. "Anytime, Hawk. Just give me a call and I'm there."

"I'll keep that in mind," he said, stepping around to open the door for her.

The mare Bri had decided to call Chocolate

stood waiting, the reins draped over the rail near the porch. Hawk had fastened the saddlebags in place.

"That should keep you till you catch up with Tanner…or until you're forced to give up the hunt for him and return here."

"That's not going to happen, Hawk. I fully intend to find Mr. Tanner Wolfe, big, bad hunter." Circling around to the left side of the animal, Bri shoved her boot into the stirrup, grasped the saddle pommel and swung herself up and over the mare, settling into the well-worn seat. Leaning forward, she stroked the mare's neck.

"Well, I see you know your way around horses," Hawk drawled, grinning back at her.

"I should. I've been around them since I was a kid, riding, grooming and, yes, even mucking stalls."

He laughed. "I don't think you'll have to do that on this trip." Then he sobered. "Reminds me— there's a sack of oats in the one bag, to supplement whatever grazing she can find, and food for Boyo."

Now Bri felt her cheeks flush with chagrin. "Thank you. I should have thought of their feed."

Hawk failed in covering a grin. "That's okay. You were a mite upset."

"No, I was a lot upset," Bri said, owning up to her anger. Gathering the reins, she thanked her host again. "I appreciate both your hospitality and your help."

"You're welcome." He tipped his hat. "Now time's a-wastin'," he chided, giving a light smack to the mare's rump. "Go, Boyo. Find Tanner."

The dog shot ahead of the horse to lead the way, beginning to weave back and forth, searching out Tanner's scent.

With a final wave to Hawk, Bri set the horse at a trot, following Boyo's lead. He quickly found the scent and settled into a lope. Keeping him in sight, Bri loped along behind him.

The day was long. Despite the bright sunshine, in the higher elevations the air was cool. It was a beautiful day to ride, but Bri wasn't riding for pleasure. She was on the hunt for two men. With any luck at all, she'd find Tanner first. Bri still felt angry but also eager, anxious and a bit scared, as well.

She had trekked the plains and jungles, the savannas and all types of mountains. Through it all, she had never felt the deep expectation and thrill of the hunt her father and his hunting buddies savored. After a while, she'd decided that one mountain looked pretty much like another, some smaller, some higher.

But this mountain, this hunt, were different. She had never hunted alone. Not going out alone was the first tenet her father had drummed into her.

Now she was on her own, trailing a dog, her sole companion. Boyo was following the scent a small distance from a stream. Made sense; Tanner and Minnich would need water.

Having eaten a solid breakfast, Bri kept going until past midafternoon. By then, she was glad to dismount and stretch. After rubbing down Chocolate, she dropped a handful of oats near a patch of grass. Next it was Boyo's turn. She scratched his head and under his long jaw and then put out the dried food Hawk had provided for him.

It was only then Bri took care of her needs. Digging into the backpack she had dropped to the ground, she pulled out a hand towel and headed toward the sound of the stream.

The rushing water foamed white around the bigger stones in the streambed. Clutching the limb of a pine tree, she lowered herself to her knees at the edge of the bank.

The water was as cold as the snow it had been at the higher elevations. Scooping handfuls, Bri cleaned her hands, rinsed her mouth and doused her face. The frigid splash took away her breath but refreshed her just the same. Drying her hands and face, she walked back to the animals and to what would be her makeshift camp for the night. The sun was lowering, and she had things to do before full sunset.

Entering the small clearing, Bri dragged a piece of a dead, dry log closer to the spot she had chosen for a fire. After gathering stones and placing them in a ring shape, she foraged for some kindling, which she ignited with a match. Once the twigs took flame, she fed the fire till the dry log began to burn.

Her growling stomach reminded her it was dinnertime. She searched the saddlebag to see what

Hawk had packed for her and found two bottles of water, peanut butter crackers, two apples, a sleeve of cheddar cheese and another of smoked ham.

Not too shabby, Bri thought, smiling. In fact, it was all nutritious as well as appealing. Silently thanking Hawk, she dragged a short log closer to the fire and sat down to eat.

Not knowing how long the food—or the hunt— would last, Bri ate sparingly, enjoying every bite. She allowed herself three pieces of chocolate for dessert.

Because the sun was quickly sinking, the shadows lengthening, she readied her sleeping bag a short way from the fire. By the time darkness fell, the air had turned decidedly cooler, so she'd shrugged into her jacket.

Wrapping her arms around her middle, she was assailed by a sudden feeling of loneliness. Another emotion overtook her, too. A yearning for Tanner. For his kiss.

Damn him, why had a simple kiss wound her up so tightly? Maybe because it was more—much, much more—than a simple kiss, she reluctantly acknowledged. His kiss was everything, the sun, the moon, the universe.

The rustle and howl of the night creatures interrupted her thoughts, and Bri realized it was now full darkness. She needed to sleep, to restore her energy for the hunt. After pulling off her boots and jacket, she crawled fully dressed into the sleeping bag, Boyo's impressive length stretched out beside her.

But sleep did not come. She lay awake for hours, watching the fire die down, while another fire roared inside her. The fire ignited by memories of Tanner and his kiss. She groaned and squeezed her eyes shut.

Even as sleep finally claimed her, she could taste Tanner's lips on her mouth.

Seven

A sound woke her before dawn. Shifting up onto one elbow, Bri glance around for the cause of the sound. It was Boyo, snuffling around on the ground.

"Hungry, boy?" she asked, grabbing her jacket before tossing back the bag's cover. Shivering, she pulled on the jacket, then retrieved Boyo's food and the oats for Chocolate. While the animals ate, she munched on a pack of peanut butter crackers between sips of water.

Within a half hour, Bri had everything together, Chocolate saddled and was on her way, once again trailing Boyo.

She made a brief stop around noon to give the animals as well as herself a break. Less than an hour later she was back on the trail. For the first part of their trek, they were following the stream upward. But slowly during the afternoon the ground leveled onto a fairly smooth plain. She let the horse pick her way through the trees and low brush while staying within sight of Boyo.

It was rough going. Once again, Bri stopped just past midafternoon. She was stiff and achy from being in the saddle so long. It felt wonderful just moving around on two legs.

After feeding the animals, Bri noticed Boyo beginning to roam. Certain he wouldn't go far, she visited the bushes for personal business, then strolled toward the stream to wash up.

Her foot caught on a root protruding from the grassy patch edging the low slope to the stream and she stumbled. When she regained her balance and glanced up, what she saw stopped her dead in her tracks. A man stood on the other side of the stream. He had changed his hair color and was wearing glasses, but Bri recognized him at once. Jay Minnich. In his hand he held a rifle hanging next to his thigh. And he was looking straight at her.

Even at that distance she could see the sick intent in his eyes. She took two steps back. He took three steps into the water, raising the rifle to his shoulder.

Bri froze. A lump of fear closed her throat, preventing her from crying out, although who she would have cried for she didn't know.

Yes, she did.

For Tanner. Where was he now, miles and miles away?

Barely breathing, Bri took another careful step back. His finger curled around the trigger. Shutting her eyes tight, she steeled herself for the impact of a bullet slamming into her body.

In that instant, not a bullet but another body slammed into her, knocking the breath completely out of her and sending the two of them to the ground. Her eyes flew open as the report from the rifle rang out and the zinging sound of a bullet whizzed overhead, a few feet above their bodies.

Tanner. She could have wept with relief, but her glance caught sight of his outstretched arm, a pistol grasped in his hand. He fired a shot, so close it sounded like a cannon blast to Bri. He gave a stern command to Boyo to stay.

Then he was up and splashing through the water. He halted about halfway across the stream to call Boyo to him. The big dog leaped into the water, crossing to the other side with Tanner. Bri could see him talk and motion to the dog, and as if in perfect understanding, Boyo sniffed the ground for a few minutes, then came to a quivering stop, head high, looking forward.

Bri knew Boyo had caught the scent of the man. Together, man and dog splashed back to her.

"He's gone," Tanner said, reaching a hand to her to help her stand. He lit into her the minute she was upright. "What in hell do you think you're doing?" He didn't give her time to reply but yelled on. "Are you trying to get yourself killed?"

Bri wet her dust-dry lips, almost as frightened of him as she had been of Minnich. "I was trying to catch up to you."

"Yeah, well, it's a damn good thing Boyo found me." He heaved a heavy exhale. "If he hadn't…" He trailed off, shuddering at the mere thought of the possible consequences.

"I won't say I'm sorry," she said, angling her chin in defiance. "I mean about tracking after you."

He sighed again. "I never expected you to." He turned away. "Let's go."

She hesitated. "Go where?"

"To my camp, of course, before it gets pitch-dark." He raised an arrogant-looking brow. "Or would you rather spend the night here?"

"No." She shook her head and made tracks to follow him when he strode away.

As Bri hadn't really unpacked anything but the food for the animals, very little time was required to get her gear together. She was in the saddle, trailing Tanner, as the sun slid toward the horizon.

His camp was surprisingly close to where she herself had stopped. Tanner had it set up, a fire going in a stone-ringed pit. A three-man domed sleeper tent was set up to one side. A log much like the one Bri had found the night before had been rolled near to the warmth of the fire.

"Home away from home," she said softly, sure he wouldn't hear her. He did.

"Yeah," he drawled a bit sarcastically. "Only we're not on vacation. You shouldn't be here at all."

"But I am, so deal with it," she retorted every bit as sarcastically. "As I told you I would be. You can't say I didn't give you an option."

"Okay, let's forget it. You're here and that's that." He turned to the fire pit. "Could you use a cup of coffee?"

"Oh, yes." She sighed. "I'd love one. But I have to wash up before it gets dark."

"I'll have the coffee and supper ready when you get back."

"Thank you." She made a beeline for the stream, energized by the promise of hot coffee and food.

After two days on the trail she felt so uncomfortable she stripped to the buff and rinsed herself all over, sorry she hadn't brought her shower wash with her. Freezing but refreshed, she rubbed herself dry and quickly dressed, unfortunately in her same clothes. She practically ran back to the camp to warm herself by the fire.

Tanner was nowhere in sight when she entered the campsite.

"Ah, there you are," he said, ducking his head as he exited the tent. "Hungry?"

"Starving," Bri admitted, hearing a low rumble in her stomach at the mention of food. "What can I do to help?"

"Not a thing," he answered, moving to the fire to stir a pot set on one of the flatter rocks. "Everything's under control."

"So I see." Bri glanced around the site. "How did you get it together so quickly?"

Tanner looked up. "I had started it when Boyo dashed into camp, to clamp his teeth onto my shirt and tug at me to follow him. Somehow I knew he was urging me on to find you." He actually smiled at her.

"Hmm," Bri murmured vaguely, her attention centered on the fluttery sensation his smile caused inside her more than on his explanation.

"How does soup sound for supper?"

"What?" Bri blinked herself out of bemusement. "Oh, soup, yes, that sounds good. What kind?"

"Vegetable. Hawk sent it along. It's dried but good. I've had it on other hunts. It shouldn't take much longer to get hot."

"You said something about coffee?" she reminded him.

"Yeah, there's some left in the thermos. Help yourself."

Bri wet her lips in anticipation, thrilling to the way Tanner's gaze followed her tongue. "Thanks." The last word came out in a dry croak that had more to do with Tanner's hot-eyed gaze than thirst.

He stood very still for a moment, staring into her eyes, then moved abruptly, striding for the gear to dig out the thermos when he realized she had no idea where it was. Pouring out a small stream of the coffee into the metal lid cup, he set it on the flat rock next to the soup pan. "Only take a minute."

The dry sound of his voice made Bri feel a little less vulnerable. Apparently she wasn't the only one affected by their proximity.

It was twilight by the time they ate their soup with chunks of dry day-old bread. For dessert, Bri took out her stash of chocolate and counted out four pieces each, to Tanner's obvious amusement.

As night began to fall, tension was a living entity between them. Every nerve in Bri's body quivered in a mixture of expectation and trepidation.

"There's a little coffee left. Would you like it?" Tanner watched her over the rim of his cup.

"Yes, please," she answered, grateful for an excuse to prolong the time to turn in. "What about Minnich?" she asked. "Do you think he might have crossed the stream with the idea that we would do the same?" Before he could reply, she rushed on, "I'd think he knows we're looking for him. What do you think?"

Tanner handed her the hot coffee before answering. "I think you're right."

Taking a careful sip, Bri nodded, swallowed. "So, then, how do we proceed? Do we cross the stream?"

He gave a quick shake of his head. "No. That's what he'll think we will do. We'll find out whether or not he crossed." His voice was mild, his tone confident.

Bri wasn't that certain. "How?"

"Boyo's got his scent. If he's crossed the stream, the dog will pick up his trail. And if he doesn't cross, he'll still follow it, because he knows damn well he'll need water."

"Of course." Bri felt like a dullard. Hadn't she seen Boyo finding the scent? Her only excuse was that she was so tense, so shaky inside about the deepening night, she wasn't thinking clearly. She lingered over the quickly cooling drink, drawing out the inevitable for as long as she possibly could. But she could procrastinate only so long.

Tanner stood up. "It's getting late," he said, stretching his arms over his head, giving her a peek at the ripple of his shoulder and chest muscles displayed by his open jacket.

Bri shivered. It was time for them to crawl into the tent. Would he expect a replay of their first wild and lingering kiss of two nights ago?

Did she want that to happen again?

Yes.

No.

At the moment she was too scared to decide. She ached from wanting his kiss, wanting him. But he was becoming too important to her, his smile, his laughter, all of him too necessary.

Tanner spoke, jarring her out of her introspection. "I'll clear away here and take care of the fire. You crawl into the tent and get undressed. I'll be with you shortly."

Bri froze for an instant. Undressed? Now was the time to tell him she wouldn't…she couldn't…

"Brianna, don't freak on me." His voice was soft, soothing. "I give you my word I won't try anything you tell me you don't want."

"Yes, but—"

"Sweetheart, I have some control," he said, shaking his head at her suspicious expression. "All I intend to do is sleep."

"But you said get undressed." Skepticism colored her tone and shaded her eyes.

"Down to your underwear. You do have long underwear, don't you?

"Yes." Bri hesitated another moment, staring into his eyes. Seeing nothing but caring there, she gave in with a quick nod and slipped inside the tent.

The interior was dimly lit by a small battery-operated lantern. The tent was roomy, plenty big enough for the two of them. But her breath caught when she looked at the sleeping bags already laid out for them. Tanner had zipped them together into one large sleeping area.

Oh, jeez.

"Brianna, I'm not going to be asking for anything you're not willing to freely give. Not now, not ever," he called to her as if somehow he knew she stood there, stock-still, staring at the bags. "Deal?"

"Y-yes," she said, carefully laying her rifle and handgun along one side of the sleeping bag, as he had placed his weapons on the other side. Then she raised her hands to her blouse to begin unbuttoning it. It was sheer relief to get out of her trail-grimy clothes. Naked, she picked up the damp towel she had used to dry off at the stream and rubbed her body down once more. Now she felt much cleaner. Tossing the towel aside, she dug into her pack for her long underwear.

Bri was snuggled inside the surprisingly roomy and comfortable bed of sleeping bags when Tanner lifted the flap and stepped inside, ushering Boyo in after him. Murmuring, "Down, boy," he pulled the zipper around the opening, enclosing the three of them inside.

Bri lifted her head. "Boyo is going to sleep in here with us?" She recognized the relieved tone in her voice.

Tanner's smile told her he recognized it, as well. "Yeah, it's getting cold out there and will likely get a lot colder by morning." With that, he began to undress.

Brianna's eyes flew wide, and he laughed out loud. "Don't panic. I'm only stripping to my underwear, and it's long underwear."

"I have silk." The words slipped out without thought. Bri was appalled at herself. She had sounded like a snit, the spoiled brat he had called her.

This time Tanner roared with laughter. "Okay, big deal. So have I."

Embarrassed, Bri turned onto her side, away from him, groaning softly at the sheer warmth, comfort and sense of protection she was feeling. In the next instant, she stiffened when his body slipped in beside her in the makeshift bed.

"Relax, kid, I'm not going to attack you."

She laughed; she couldn't help it. He sounded oh so amused beneath his serious tones. "I'm glad to hear it. I wouldn't want to have to hurt you."

His laughter was drowned out by Boyo, who stood, whining.

"I think he needs to go out," Bri said.

"No kidding," he grumbled. Getting up, he shrugged into his jacket, pulled on his boots. "Okay, okay," he said to the dog. "I'm coming." Unzipping the flap, he let Boyo outside. Pausing at the opening, he said, "I may as well check on the mare while I'm out."

"Chocolate."

He turned to stare at her through the dim lantern light. "You want chocolate now?"

"No." Bri had to laugh this time. "The mare. I've temporarily given her the name Chocolate, as I never asked Hawk what her real name is."

"Oh." He dipped his head and exited the tent. She heard his chuckle as he walked away.

Tanner was gone for some ten or so minutes, during which Bri shimmied around inside the sleeping bags. Once again she turned onto her side, this time facing the side he'd been sleeping on.

When Tanner did return, he zipped up the opening and shrugged out of his jacket and boots.

After turning around in a circle several times,

Boyo settled down across the opening of the tent. If anyone tried to enter during the night, they were going to have to walk over the big dog to do so.

Bri smiled at the very idea of anyone getting past the wolfhound and living to tell about it, possibly even if that someone were a bear. Her thoughts scattered when Tanner, smiling with her, slid in next to her.

"Are you warm enough?"

She nodded. The bed warmed her skin, but Tanner's smile warmed her body inside and out. "What are you doing?" she blurted when he drew her close to him, cradling her in his arms.

"I just want to hold you, Brianna," he said, his breath fluttering over her forehead. "Comfortable?"

"Hmm," she murmured, snuggling closer, so close she could feel his chuckle before she heard it.

"Good. Sleepy?"

"Not really," Bri said, stifling a yawn. "I'm just happy to stretch out, be warm and relaxed and off the back of a horse for a while."

This time he laughed aloud. Bri loved the sound of his laughter. It seemed to surround her with a sense of warmth and security.

"So you're not as tough as you thought you were," Tanner said, teasing her.

"Yes, I am," Bri said, pulling her head back to glare at him. "It's simply that I haven't been on a horseback trek in some time. I can handle it. It's only a little stiffness."

"I never doubted it." Tanned did his best to look serious. The gleam in his eyes gave him away.

"Yeah, right." She scowled.

He laughed again, cupped her head to draw her face closer to his and planted a gentle kiss on her temple. "I really didn't doubt it, Brianna."

Bri melted. She loved the way he said her name. "Okay, you're forgiven." Her temple was tingling where his lips had touched.

"Thank you." Laughter danced along his voice. "Is that a blanket forgiveness, covering my having left Hawk's without you?"

She hesitated long moments, smothering the anger she had been nursing since she had discovered him gone. "I suppose so," she said, giving in, but only because she really wanted to do so.

"Grudging, but I'm grateful for it."

They were quiet a moment, his breath teasing her skin, sending tingles from her temple to every nerve ending in her body. Desperately hanging on to her desire to have him kiss her, maybe make love to her, Bri raked her mind for something to say to break the feeling of sensual intimacy curling around them, seemingly drawing them closer to the precipice of no return.

To defuse the volatile intimacy, she said, "Tell me about yourself, Tanner, your life." Her voice sounded ragged even to her own ears.

"Why do I have this sneaky suspicion you don't trust me?" His tone was drily amused.

"It—it's not that," she said. "I do trust you." Bri realized she truly did, that she would trust him with her life. Odd, she mused, after having known him such a short amount of time. But there it was. Then again, he had saved her life only hours ago.

"If it's not that," he said, "what is it?"

"Me." Bri's throat felt suddenly parched. "It's myself I don't trust, Tanner."

"I don't get it." He sounded more than a little confused. "You don't trust yourself about what?"

Once again Bri hesitated, unsure if she should explain her feelings. "You. I don't trust myself with you," she admitted, glancing up at him, her confidence bolstered by the fact that his face was in the shadows.

She could feel his body go completely still, feel the tautness in his arms around her. What must he be thinking? Had she unwittingly insulted him?

Frustration was sharp in his voice when he spoke. "Brianna, I told you, I won't—"

"No, Tanner, please listen. You don't understand," she said, burrowing closer to him. "I know *you* won't." She sighed. "The problem is I'm not sure *I* won't."

"I see." Enclosing her again in his arms, this time even more tightly, he kissed her ear, whispering, "You know something, Brianna? You're a little nuts."

No one had ever said anything like that to her before. Her reaction began with a giggle and grew from there to laughter that spilled out from deep inside. Burying her face in the curve of his neck, she laughed harder than she could recall having laughed in a very long time. Partly because she thought it funny and partly in sheer relief.

"You know something, Tanner?" she gasped through her dying laughter. "You're right."

His lips brushed her cheek. "That's okay, kid, because I'm a bit nuts, too."

Eight

She loved this man. The realization flashed through her mind like a sudden bolt of lightning.

Bri's insides seized. What was she thinking? Love? She couldn't have fallen in love this quickly. Could she? Abruptly her laughter died in her throat, but she kept her face pressed against his shoulder, inhaling the spicy, male scent of him.

"Amuse you, do I?" Tanner asked, laughter dancing on his own voice. "I really didn't think it was all that funny."

"Oh, Tanner, you have no idea." Bri had to pause to take a breath, collect herself, get her thoughts back in line. "That's one of the reasons I don't trust myself with you. You're so up-front and straightforward. So few people are today, it's refreshing to find someone who is." She was chattering, making it up as she rattled on, determinedly blanking all thoughts of Minnich and the L word from her mind. At least that's what she told herself.

"Despite your PC phrasing, why do I get the idea you're impugning my gender?"

Bri couldn't help it; she smiled. If he had been trying to sound offended, he had failed completely.

"I'll plead the Fifth," she said, shooting a quick look at him.

"Right now I wish I *had* a fifth."

At that, her laughter erupted. Even Boyo lifted his head at the happy sound of it.

Within seconds, Tanner joined her. The sound was music to Bri's ears.

"What exactly are we laughing at, do you know?" he asked as his laughter subsided.

"At ourselves, I think," she answered, drawing a deep, sobering breath. "It was fun, though, wasn't it?"

"Yeah." Tanner was quiet a moment, doing some deep breathing of his own. "What do you want to know?"

"What?" His sudden question threw her.

"You said before that you wanted to know more about me," he said. "So what do you want to know?"

"Everything." The word burst out before she could hold it back.

"Oh, is that all?" He lifted one shoulder in a half

shrug. "That should take no longer than…oh, five, six hours. Of course, if I remember correctly, we went over our respective favorite things at lunch in Durango. Didn't we?"

"Yes, I know, but I meant…well, other things."

"Like what?"

"Have you ever been in love?" Oh, damn, why was she having trouble with that darn *love* word? Nevertheless, she waited, not breathing, for his answer. If he would answer.

He didn't hesitate. "I thought I was once." His shoulder shrugged and she breathed again. "I was wrong. Have you?"

Bri wouldn't allow herself to be less candid than Tanner. She even took it a step further. "Once. I was wrong, too. He was a handsome, charming snake, a cheat and a user."

"Gee, could you be a bit more specific?" he said, his voice teasing.

"He was a rat," she said, deadly serious. "I came back to the dorm one night from the library to find him in bed with my roommate. I threw him out first. Then, without a shred of remorse, I used my father's influence to get her out of the room and into another dorm."

"You are tough."

"I was mad." Memory anger colored her voice. "At least I didn't do either one of them bodily injury."

"I'm glad to hear it," he said. "For an instant there I was afraid you were going to tell me you punched her out and took a skinning knife to him."

"Son of a gun," Bri deadpanned. "Why didn't I think of that at the time?"

Tanner let go of a smile right before he brushed his lips over her mouth. "Next question?"

His breath bathed her lips, stole her breath, tangled her thoughts.

"Did you fall asleep?" His lips were now at her ear again, teasing, tormenting.

"No." It was barely a croak.

"Are you out of questions?"

"No, I'm…thinking."

"Does it hurt?" His tone was solicitous.

She gave him a look.

He grinned, unrepentant. "We could discuss favorite holidays. Mine's Thanksgiving. The turkey and trimmings, you know. Anything else?"

"Well…" She hesitated a moment, then took the plunge. "I was wondering about Candy."

He frowned. "The dark chocolate you've been doling out like it was gold?" He licked his lips, stirring a wish inside Bri that it were her lips being laved. "I love it, the darker the better."

"No." Bri shook her head in an attempt to shake off the sudden need of his mouth and quickly asked, "Would you like some now?"

"No, thank you." He chuckled. "Was that one of your questions?"

"No, and I think you know it," she said, suspicion growing. "I mean Candy of the Hamptons."

"What about her?" She could almost hear his frown in his voice.

"She seemed...oh, I don't know, kind of possessive of you. Are you...?"

"I believe I answered that at the time, Brianna." Impatience rode his tone. "There is not now, nor has there ever been, anything personal between us."

"I'm sorry." Bri was quick to back off. "I know it's none of my business."

He sighed. "There is no business so far as Candy is concerned. I'm not interested in her the way you mean."

"Personally, sexually?" Bri asked boldly.

"No, sweetheart, I'm not. Wouldn't do me any good if I were. She's engaged to the man who was waiting for her in the restaurant. Besides, she's not my type. Too forward, too easy."

Bri frowned. "What does that mean?"

"What you think it means. She's been with too many men. Not that it's any of my business. But I'm a lot more particular than some other men."

Satisfaction swept through Bri like balm. "I think I knew that."

She knew he shook his head as if in puzzlement, not only because she felt the motion but also because the strands of his long hair brushed against her cheek and tickled her neck.

"If you knew, why ask?"

Bri scoured her mind for a reasonable or at least plausible answer. "Uh...I'm nosy?"

"And a lousy liar," he retorted. "You wanted to know because you didn't like her on sight and thought asking me how I felt about her would give you some idea about my character—or lack of same."

Smart-ass. Bri kept the instant thought inside her head, where it belonged. But, of course, he was right, so she supposed she might as well admit it.

"Yes," she confessed, not at all contrite.

"Sneaky, Brianna," he chided her, amusement lacing his tone. "Clever but sneaky."

"Obviously not too clever," she said wryly. "You were on to me at once."

"Okay, then I'm clever." He pulled her even closer to him.

"Yes, you are," she said, trying and failing to swallow a yawn.

"Sleepy?" he murmured.

"Yes," she answered, thinking it was pointless to deny what had to be apparent to him.

"Twenty Questions over for tonight?"

"I suppose." She sighed. "Except…what's your favorite color?"

"Well, it used to be blue, like in jeans," he answered. "But now it's auburn-red, like the gorgeous color of your hair."

Said hair quivered at the back of Bri's neck. "Thank you." Her voice quivered, too. She was losing ground here, and fast. Bri knew if she didn't call a halt now, she could happily whistle goodbye to her need for sleep for some time.

"What's yours?"

Huh? Bri frowned in the dimness. Oh, her favorite color! What the heck was it? Biding for time to remember what should be obvious to her, she stifled a fake yawn against his neck.

"Don't lose sleep over it." His voice was both soft and tender. "You may answer and resume your third degree of me on the trail tomorrow."

Bri heaved a deep sigh of relief.

He chuckled.

Bri sighed heavier, wishing he wouldn't do that. "Oh, did you have to mention that? I was trying to forget I would have to get back on the horse tomorrow."

"You'll do just fine and you know it."

"Yes." She yawned again and stopped fighting her heavy eyelids. "Good night, Tanner."

"Warm and comfortable?"

"Deliciously." Her voice was slurring.

He chuckled. "Then go to sleep."

"Okay." The next instant, Bri was out. She never heard him say good-night to her.

As he had two nights before at Hawk's place, Tanner lay awake for a long time after Brianna fell asleep, breathing in the smell of herbal shampoo in her hair, the elusive natural woman scent. It was a heady aroma, pure female, delicious. He'd love to taste her.

He drew another, deeper breath, trying to calm

his senses. All it accomplished was to arouse them and him even more.

He lost himself in the fantasy of the smooth softness of Brianna's skin as he moved his hands over her body. How he had wanted to caress her, kiss her, every inch of her, hold her close to his hard body.

He wanted her so badly, ached to be deep inside of her, become a part of her. Everything inside him clenched with need, and he pressed his lips together to contain the groan swelling his throat.

Damn. He needed to get away from her, if only for a few minutes. He needed to get out of the tent, into the air. Maybe the chill of night would cool his overheated body, his hungry thoughts.

Stealthily he slid from the makeshift bed. Hushing Boyo, he unzipped the door and slipped into the night.

The air was chilly but not cool enough. Tanner thought what he really needed was a cold shower. The stream. Without another thought, he grabbed a towel from one of the packs and was moving through the forest, along the path, following the sound of water. He hadn't gone very far when Boyo loped up to pace protectively alongside him.

"You should have stayed with Brianna, boy," he murmured. "I can take care of myself."

As if understanding Tanner's every word, the dog slowed to a near stop, cocking his large head to look up at him, waiting, watching.

"I'll be okay." Tanner's voice took on a hint of

command. "Go back, boy, make sure she's safe in the tent."

A second of hesitation, then the dog turned to trot back the way he had come.

Shaking his head in wonder of the animal's obvious intelligence, Tanner continued on to the creek. The water wasn't merely cool or even cold; it felt like melted ice, which was very close to what it actually was.

Pulling off his underwear, Tanner briskly waded into the stream. He caught his breath at the shock of the freezing water and, holding it inside him, he lay out flat to submerge his entire body.

He lasted all of a couple seconds before scrambling up and onto the bank. Scooping up the towel, he swiftly and roughly dried his shivering and thankfully no longer aroused body. Pulling on his underwear, he made his way back to the protection of the tent, the warmth of the bed…and the woman asleep in it.

Shivering almost violently, he slid between the layers of the sleeping bag, close to her warmth but not touching her until his underwear warmed and his body stopped shivering.

Sighing with relief and moving slowly so as not to wake her, he reached to the side to turn off the lamp but hesitated for just a few moments to gaze into her face. Smiling, he switched off the lamp.

Beautiful, beautiful, he thought, settling close to her again, her face nestled in the curve of his neck.

Awake, laughing, somber, Brianna was beautiful. Asleep, she was even more so. She was exquisite.

She sighed and her warm breath fluttered over his skin. Tanner felt a twist in his chest. What was it about this particular woman that could make him ache, not only with desire but with admiration, caring and an urgent need to protect?

He had known many women, some intimately, some as pals, friends. He had cared for them, each and every one of them. He had even begun to believe he was in love with one of them. Yet none had ever affected him with the depth of feelings and emotion as Brianna.

"What is it about you?" Tanner whispered. Once again that twist curled in his chest. The descriptive word hovered in his mind, waiting to be recognized.

Love.

Tanner froze, rejecting the very concept. Love? He hardly knew her. And he had never believed in the fairy tales of love at first sight and happily ever after. He wasn't sure he believed in love at all.

No, he wasn't in love with Brianna. He couldn't be. Not so quickly. Could he?

She made a murmuring sound—not a sigh but not an actual word, either—and snuggled closer to him. Was she cold? The thought had him drawing her tightly to his once again warm body.

Then she sighed. Her eyelids fluttered, and she softly kissed the side of his neck. Tanner stilled. Was she awake or nuzzling him in her sleep?

"Tanner…"

Her voice was soft but not sleepy.

"I'm here," he answered.

"Will you kiss me?"

Everything went still inside him. Would he? He was dying with wanting to kiss her, make love with her. "If that's what you want," he whispered against her ear.

"Yes…" She murmured the word on a sigh and lifted her head, offering her mouth to him.

He gratefully accepted, claiming her lips with his own. Her mouth was sheer heaven and made him burn like the fires of hell. Tanner deepened the kiss, wanting, needing, desperate for more of the sweet, erotic taste of her mouth.

Brianna returned his kiss with a hunger that scorched him. The heat spread through his body, making him hard. With the last of his common sense, Tanner told himself to end it at once, before it was too late. But he had tuned out reason, not paying a bit of attention. Instead his mouth delved deeper into hers, savoring the nectar that was exclusively Brianna's.

Getting desperate, Tanner shifted his hips to bring his body against hers, letting her feel his arousal, his desire to be one with her.

Instead of withdrawing, as he was certain she would, she tightened her arms around him and, clinging to his mouth, ground her hips against his, inflaming him more, burning his common sense to ashes.

"Brianna." His voice was raw, roughened by passion whirling out of control.

"Yes." That was all she said. That was all she needed to say. The needy arch of her hips into his said the rest.

"Are you sure?" He had to know now, before he went up in flames.

Brianna remained silent but answered by moving away from him. Tanner went cold, then immediately hot again as she sat up and pulled her top over her head, tossing it aside to land atop her weapons.

Tanner was tempted to laugh for an instant, thinking the most dangerous weapons were right there, in the form of her satiny skin, her beautiful breasts, her puckering nipples.

He sucked in a breath, aching to suck on her, taste the offering she made to him. He leaned forward to her, disappointment streaking through him when she moved away from him.

What the hell? The thought was a wisp, gone when he saw her wiggling out of her pants. His body throbbing with lust for her, he jackknifed upright and shucked out of his underwear.

At the same moment he slipped back into the sleeping bag, she opened her thighs in invitation. Tanner was not about to refuse. As he slid between her legs, thrilling to the silkiness of her skin, he captured one nipple and sucked it into his hungry mouth.

He thought he could feast on her forever, but he was wrong. It soon became obvious Brianna would not simply lie there like a sacrifice. She ran her hands all over his body, his chest, his back, his hips, his belly, his...

"*Brianna.*" His voice was ragged with strain. He exerted every ounce of control to hold back, just kissing her, caressing her, giving her the utmost enjoyment.

She was having none of his restraint. Releasing him, she drew him up and over her, seeking his mouth. "Don't wait, Tanner," she whispered against his lips. "I need you inside me now."

Happy to comply, he moved into position and thrust his tongue into her mouth at the same instant he slid his body into hers.

She gasped. For a moment he froze, afraid he had somehow hurt her, but she grasped his hips, digging her nails into his flesh and arching her hips as she pulled him deeper into her body.

Tanner went wild. Still hanging on to a shred of control, he began to move, slowly, then faster, deeper. She moaned, arching high into each successive thrust, driving him on yet holding back until, crying out, she soared over the edge of utter pleasure. Tension became nearly unbearable inside him. He gave one final thrust and he was there, soaring with her in the most incredible completion of his life.

Bri lay beside him, her heart racing, her breathing harsh, her body sated and depleted. Never, never had she experienced anything so mind-shattering, so earthshaking, so absolutely wonderful. She wanted to laugh and cry at the same time. It had been so very beautiful.

"Are you all right?" Tanner's voice was close to her ear, soft with concern. He lay beside her, his own breathing labored.

"Oh, Tanner," she answered between gasped breaths. "That was so…so…"

"Yes, it was," he murmured, kissing her earlobe. "It was even more than that."

She sighed with satisfaction. "Thank you."

"Me?" He sounded astounded. "I should be thanking you. Brianna, you are magnificent."

Turning her head, she brushed her lips over his, whispering, "Yeah, I am, ain't I?"

Tanner laughed. Then he was kissing her, her temple, her cheek, her chin and, finally, her lips. Her lips clinging to his, she drowned in his mouth.

Minutes later, curled against him, her head pillowed on his perspiration-slick chest, safe and secure in the cradle of Tanner's arms, Brianna fell asleep. All thoughts of tomorrow had been swept from her mind by the release of her tension from their lovemaking.

Tanner lay awake, his mind playing with the idea of him and Brianna being, staying together. No, he thought. Damn. There was no way he could be with her. When their hunt was over, she would go home to Pennsylvania, her quiet library, her upper-class friends. He, on the other hand, would be here. Or there. Or wherever he needed to go, hunting down criminals for money.

They had had great sex one time. No, he corrected, they had made love one time. But one time did not make a relationship.

Brianna was above him.

Tanner shook his head. That was wrong. Her father may have more money than his folks, but that didn't put her above him…not in any way other than where he placed her. In his mind he placed her if not on a pedestal then as the most important person in his life. And he knew, without doubt, if necessary he would lay down his life to protect her.

Why the hell did he bring her along instead of dragging her back to Hawk's place? Certainly not for the money. He had already decided not to take anything from her. In truth, he really didn't need the money—he liked it, but he didn't need it. He had earned plenty enough in his chosen occupation and he had invested the bulk of it wisely. While Tanner wasn't wealthy, he had a very comfortable nest egg.

But money didn't have anything to do with his situation concerning Brianna.

Although she was experienced in the hunt, it was this hunt and this hunt only she cared about, and with good reason. She had told him she no longer liked trekking, even with a camera. She had an altogether different lifestyle in the world of books and normal activities.

Tanner felt certain Brianna considered his lifestyle abnormal. So where did that leave them when the hunt was over? He knew the answer. It left her on the East Coast and him in Colorado or parts unknown.

Brianna moved closer to him, one long leg sliding over his thigh. Tanner's body hardened in response. Grimacing in discomfort, he drew a deep breath, exerting control. It wasn't easy, but he shifted back an inch, away from temptation. The need raging inside him subsided a little and he released a long sigh of relief.

He ordered his body, his emotions, to forget the ifs and might-have-beens and focus on the long day ahead.

His inner voice had one piece of advice. Go the hell to sleep.

Nine

The first pale light of predawn tinged the horizon when Tanner woke her.

"Brianna," he said softly. "It's time to roll out. You have enough time to dress and wash up before the coffee's ready."

"Mmm," she answered. Kind of.

Tanner chuckled. "Is that an 'okay' or a 'get lost'?"

The warm sound of his soft laughter tingled Bri into full wakefulness. She yawned before saying, "Okay, I'll be out in a few minutes."

She was true to her word…almost. It was a little more than a few minutes, more like eight or ten, and two of those minutes were used up simply getting her tired body out of the sleeping bag. Once she was upright, Bri pulled on jeans and a shirt over her long underwear and clean socks before pulling on her boots. By the time she finished, the soreness in her body from having sex after so long a time had eased to a mild ache.

After using her toiletries and pulling her hair back into a ponytail, she repacked her bag and carted it outside. She dropped it next to Tanner's, then made a dash for the bushes.

His soft chuckle followed after her. Trying her best to ignore a tingle in response to him, she concentrated on the urgent business at hand.

Finished, she cleaned her hands on a toss-away sanitary wipe, then followed the aroma of coffee back to camp.

She found Tanner squatting over the fire, preparing two cups of instant coffee. He held one up to her and she took it.

As he worked to put out the fire, his muscular thighs stretched the denim of his jeans, reminding her of how impressive they'd felt against her last night. When he looked up and she saw his face behind the curtain of his dark hair, she remembered how his eyes had looked down at her with passion. She promptly dropped her cup.

Boyo jumped up, barking at the sound of the tin cup hitting a rock. Taking up the charge, the horses whinnied and restlessly moved.

"Now look what you've done," Tanner said, standing. "You've gone and spooked the animals."

"S-sorry, I don't know what happened. I'm not usually clumsy." Nor did she usually get affected like that by a man.

Tanner handed Bri his own coffee and, after calming down Boyo, went to settle the horses.

Bri watched his easy gait, his tight rear, and once again felt unsteady. She had to force her eyes away from his body and onto the horses. From a sack he'd pulled out of the pack, he sprinkled some feed on the ground for the two horses. His diversion worked. The horses went immediately to their feed.

He was impressive with the animals. Gentle, firm when needed but always attentive, just as he'd been last night with Boyo in the tent.

And with her, said an inner voice.

She managed to ignore the images that thought conjured.

"We've got to eat and get going," Tanner told her when he returned to the fire. "I'm sure Minnich isn't out there lingering over breakfast." Before she could agree, he handed her an oatmeal bar.

She was so hungry she downed it before Tanner had the fire out.

When he got up and noticed her empty wrapper, he seemed surprised. "Would you like another one?"

Embarrassed, she looked up at him from underneath her lashes. "If we have enough."

Chewing his own bar, he retrieved another and gave it to her. "We've got to get packed now."

She followed his lead, picking up her coffee cup and loading her saddlebag on Chocolate.

"Here, I'll take that." Tanner came up beside her to heft the other pack she held. "It's heavy."

"I can handle it," she said, but the words got stuck in her throat when she turned and found his face mere inches from hers. He lingered there, and, too awestruck to move, Bri drew in the scent of him. He looked even better in the light of day than he had last night.

When she found her voice, she asked, "What are you doing?"

"Me?" Tanner replied. "You're the one who was batting those long eyelashes at me before. Are they fake?"

"Fake?" Bri nearly screeched but held back to not startle the animals again. "I'll have you know, Mr. Wolfe, I have never in my life worn fake eyelashes…or anything else."

Tanner's face split in a grin. "I know. You're the real thing," he drawled as he ran a slow, heated look over her body from head to toe, allowing his eyes to travel where his hands had gone last night.

The slow burn in Tanner's eyes gave Bri a hot flash. Steadying the uneven rhythm of her breathing, she croaked out, "Is there any water?"

Without stepping far from her, he pulled a bottle out of his saddlebag. She took it and gulped a mouthful. The cold water did nothing to calm her heated thoughts. Last night had been…everything. It was as if they'd suddenly become one…one body, one soul, one completed entity. Making love with Tanner had been the best experience of her life, and she couldn't wait to do it again and again….

She couldn't stifle the gasp that rose out of her throat. Oh, Lord, she was in big-time trouble.

"Are you okay?" concern shaded Tanner's voice.

"Yes…I'm sorry," she managed to say. "The breakfast bar must have gotten stuck in my throat." At his skeptical look, she turned away, going to retrieve another pack.

Within twenty minutes they had their mounts ready, the packhorses loaded and were on the move.

They rode single file along the narrow track. When the path widened enough for two, Bri rode up alongside him.

"I've been thinking," she said. "Suppose Minnich doesn't follow the stream but moves high into the mountains?" She'd forced herself to ignore Tanner and focus on the reason they were here.

"Unless he knows exactly where there is more water, he can't afford to do that. He has food, but eventually he'll run out of that. Now he can last a good while without food, foraging for edible early-spring plants and berries. But water?" He shook his head. "The way I see it, he'll likely stay with the stream." He sent a sidelong look at her. "Naturally I could be wrong. The melting snow is filling many small streams and creeks. If he knows his way around these mountains, he'll veer off. But I'm banking he doesn't know them that well."

Bri nodded her understanding. "But I know you enough by now to be fairly sure you thought he would stay on this course. You didn't hesitate, you deliberately chose this way. Why?"

"Because this way leads into the thickest section of the wilderness, the least traveled by tourists, hikers and backpackers. And because this stream is well marked on maps of the area."

"Makes sense. I should have known better than to even ask such a stupid question."

"No." Tanner shook his head, swinging the ponytail hanging out from under the wide brim of his hat. "You can ask anything you want, Brianna. There are no stupid questions, just sometimes stupid answers."

"Somehow I don't think you give many of them."

He smiled at her compliment. Already soft, Bri's insides went all squishy. She gathered the loose reins to drop back again, but his hand snaked out, covering hers.

"Stay and ride with me, Brianna," he said, keeping a light, disturbing hold on her hand. "We'll be stopping for a rest and a quick lunch soon."

Ridiculous as it seemed, with his hand lightly resting on hers, Bri had never before enjoyed riding so much, even with the ache in her rear end settling in once again.

From her position next to him Bri could now

clearly see Boyo, moving in a wide area back and forth ahead of them, his head moving from side to side, searching.

"Boyo is a worker, isn't he?"

"Boyo comes from a line of grand champion wolfhounds." He turned to grin at her. "But he loves to hunt."

"Hawk doesn't show him?" She tried really hard to ignore the effects of his grin. It didn't work.

"Hell, no." Tanner laughed. "Can you see Hawk traipsing around a show ring, leading Boyo?"

Bri frowned. "There's nothing wrong with showing dogs. They're beautiful."

"I know," he agreed, to her surprise. "I watch the competitions on Animal Planet. But think, Brianna—can you really picture Hawk all duded up at a dog show?"

Bri tried to imagine it and soon gave up the effort. She smiled. "Not really."

"Thought so."

"Where did Hawk get Boyo?"

"He was a gift from Hawk's father."

"Is his father still alive?"

"Alive and well and raising champion wolfhounds in Scotland where he lives." He chuckled. "He gave Hawk his pick of a litter and Hawk chose Boyo. His father was delighted because Boyo was the runt and he was certain he wouldn't show well, anyway. Turns out, Boyo was the pick of the litter, the largest and the best, and would have made a great champion."

"Way to go, Boyo," Bri called, stretching her back and neck to catch a glimpse of the constantly moving dog. She winced at the pain that attacked her shoulders.

As usual, Tanner didn't miss a thing. "Need a break?" he asked, moving his hand from hers to massage her tight shoulder.

Bri sighed for betraying herself to him. She felt like a greenhorn, a feeling she didn't appreciate. "Yes," she admitted, immediately adding, "I'm sorry if I'm holding you up."

He slanted a scowl at her. "You're not holding me up, Brianna. I could use a short break, too. And I'm hungry. That wasn't exactly a filling breakfast this morning." His scowl gave way to a teasing smile. "Also, I need a cup of coffee as much as you do."

She laughed at the same time she saw her vision blur. What was she getting all misty-eyed over? She derided herself. A rush of tears just because he was being so caring and thoughtful of her? She heaved a silent sigh.

And she had asked herself if she could handle him? Dumb question, she chided herself. But then, she hadn't expected to fall in love with him, either.

Foolish woman, Bri thought, bringing the horse to a halt in the small clearing he had chosen. Only a fool would blindly go along, falling in love with a maverick.

While Tanner unpacked the things for their

lunch, Bri tried to walk out the stiffness in her legs from being in the saddle for hours. When he returned, she left him to go to the stream to wash her hands, splash water on her face.

Once again she followed the scent of coffee back to camp. But how could she smell it when he hadn't built a fire? The answer was waiting for her at the edge of the small clearing where they had stopped. Tanner was holding a steaming cup, creamer added, for her. And there was no sign of a small fire.

"How did you make that?" she asked, glancing around the clearing.

"I made extra this morning and filled one of the thermoses," he said, taking a careful sip from the cup in his other hand.

Duh. "I should have figured that out for myself," she said, blowing gently on the liquid before taking a sip. He grinned. Bri felt the beginnings of that now-familiar melting sensation inside. Giving herself a mental shake, she grinned back at him. "What's for lunch?"

"Come see. It's all ready." He led the way to the clearing, where they feasted on premade peanut butter sandwiches, apples and, of course, some chocolate.

They were back on the trail in less than an hour.

Bri hadn't been back in the saddle very long before, out of the blue, she said, "I'm sorry."

At Tanner's invitation, she was still riding alongside him. Turning slightly in his saddle, he tilted his head to give her a puzzled look.

"About what?"

She hesitated, licked her lips, then blurted out, "I realize now I shouldn't have forced you to take me with you, nor followed you when you left me at Hawk's. I'm slowing you down and I know it."

"Brianna…" he began.

She rushed on. "I haven't been on a horseback hunt in ages. Hell, other than a jog in my father's fields every so often, I haven't been on horseback at all, at least not long enough to ache." She barely paused to draw breath, not giving him time to speak, before babbling on. "Now I'm beginning to ache all over, and, and…"

"And, as I said," he quickly inserted, "you're really nuts."

He smiled, so softly, so gently, she felt a twist in her chest. "First off," he continued, "you didn't force me into anything. Trust me, sweetheart, I don't force easily. Secondly, we couldn't go any faster without wearing out the horses, especially the one packing." He smiled again, only this time his smile was sheer temptation. "And third, but most importantly, after a bit of consideration, I knew I wanted you along."

For an instant Bri's heart appeared to stop. No, everything inside her seemed to stop. "But you said—"

Once again he cut her off. "I know what I said. I changed my mind." One dark brow lifted. "Did you think only women were allowed to do that?"

"No, of course not, but—"

"Wait." Tanner brought his mount to a halt and reached out to halt her horse. "Look at Boyo."

Bri swept her gaze around, almost missing the dog standing perfectly still in the underbrush. Even from the distance separating them she could see him quivering. Boyo spotted something and was ready to spring into action.

Ten

"Stay, boy." Tanner's low command told her he knew the dog was ready to bolt for whatever it was he saw.

"It couldn't be Minnich already, could it?" Bri asked quietly. "He took off yesterday, but you had to wait for me. Could we have caught up already?"

"Yeah, but he didn't know he was being followed until yesterday, and even then he might have thought we were just packers," he answered just as quietly. "Why would we have spooked him?"

"Because you fired at him?"

"Maybe. But on the other hand, he saw you, apparently alone...."

"I was," she cut in. "At least I thought I was."

"Right, and so did he. So, yeah, it could be him. He's deep in the wilds now, likely giving himself and the horses a rest. I'm gonna have to get closer."

"We're going to get closer?"

"We are." Moving to the packhorses, he removed his gun belt from one of the packs and strapped it around his waist. Digging back into the pack, he retrieved his pistol, checked it and settled it in the holster. She couldn't miss the pair of binoculars in a pouch on the left side of the belt. Walking back to his horse, he slid his rifle from the scabbard.

Bri turned to her horse to get her own rifle.

He frowned. "Do you really think you'll need that weapon?"

"I'm taking it." She allowed him a sweet smile. "But I'll leave the pistol here."

"Wonderful." Sighing, he moved slowly, silently forward.

Boyo paced beside him on the left, while Bri matched his steps on his right. They hadn't gone very far when Tanner and Boyo came to a halt. Bri stopped next to him.

Across the stream, some distance away, she could just make out a man standing on the other side. There was a small clearing near the bank, but the horses were tethered and a makeshift camp had been set up to the back, under cover of the tall pines, surrounded by brush.

Tanner took out the field glasses. He gazed through

them a few moments, then slid them back in the pouch. "It's Minnich," he murmured, sounding positive.

Then all hell broke out, everything seemingly happening at once.

A shot rang out and Tanner's hat went flying. In unison, they dropped to the ground. Tanner scooped up his hat and poked his finger through the hole in front. Bri vaguely heard him mutter, "Son of a bitch, I thought that only happened in the movies."

With a bone-chilling yowl, Boyo took off running, as Tanner and Bri raised their rifles to their shoulders.

Another shot rang out. Boyo let out a horrible-sounding yelp and flew into the air, then crashed to the ground. At the same time, two more shots rang out. With an outcry of pain, Minnich went down.

"I got the bastard." Tanner took off at a run toward the downed man, splashing through the stream.

"I got him," Bri yelled, also running, but she was not running through the water but to Boyo.

She went cold at her first sight of the dog. He was lying still, not whining. Breath eased from Bri as she saw his chest move. He was alive.

She dropped to her knees next to him, gently running her hands over his wiry-haired body. Her hand came away wet with blood when she touched his shoulder. "*Bastard*'s too mild a word for the lowlife," she mumbled, parting Boyo's fur to examine the wound.

She sighed with relief when she saw the bleeding was not profuse, indicating a major artery hadn't been hit. But had the shell gone through his body?

Even as the thought went through her mind, Bri was carefully sliding her hand beneath Boyo, feeling for a wet spot. There was none. The bullet was still inside somewhere.

She had to stop the bleeding. Not wanting to leave him even long enough to run back to the horses for the first-aid kit, Bri yanked her shirt from her waistband, popping buttons as she pulled it off.

Without a thought that she was sitting there with only her silk long undershirt on or the chill in the air, she began tearing the shirt into strips. Folding them into pads, she lay them on the wound, applying gentle pressure. She had just changed pads when Tanner loped up to her with the first-aid kit in hand.

Sliding around to give him access to the wound, Bri gently lifted the dog's head to her lap. "You're such a brave boy," she murmured, stroking Boyo's head as Tanner poured water over the pad before carefully removing it from the wound. The dog didn't so much as whimper as Tanner dried and cleaned the ugly gash. Bri continued to soothe the animal with soft praise. "You risked your life for us, Boyo. You're a genuine hero." She stroked his head and muzzle, and every time she got close to his mouth, his long tongue flicked out to lick her hand.

"Why, thank you for the kisses," she said,

watching Tanner as he applied an antibiotic cream to the wound before pressing a sterile pad against it. Taking out a roll of gauze, he wound it around Boyo's body, anchoring the pad. Then he took out a syringe, rubbed a spot on the animal's leg with a sterilized pad and carefully slid the needle into the leg.

Bri glanced up at Tanner in question.

"For pain," he said. "I didn't want to waste time before we stopped the bleeding," he explained. "He should rest easy now." He raised his brows. "You must be uncomfortable. Do you want me to move him?"

"No, no, I'm fine." It was a bald-faced lie. Bri was aching all over now, partly from tension, but there was no way she was letting him move the injured dog away from her.

Tanner smiled as if he'd known her answer before asking the question. "Okay. I've notified Hawk. He and a rescue helicopter will be here in a couple of hours."

Bri frowned. "How did you reach Hawk?"

He smiled again, teasingly. "It's called a cell/walkie-talkie phone."

She gave him a narrow-eyed look. Then suddenly she remembered. "Minnich. Did you get him?"

Tanner nodded. "Took a couple of bullets, but he's still alive. I carried him back to our horses. He's in a lot of pain, so I tied him up real tight. Make him suffer for what he's done."

Seemingly picking up on her inner turmoil, Boyo licked her hand as if comforting her. "Do you think he might be thirsty?" she asked, nodding down at the dog.

"Probably." Tanner nodded, handing her the thermos he had used to clean the wound. "There's still some water in here. He can't get up, but you can lift his head enough so he can lap up some of it."

Bri was already pouring the cool liquid into the small cup and slowly lifting his head. "Come on, Boyo, help me here. You've got to be thirsty after all you've been through." She barely noticed Tanner turning away.

"I'm going to check on Minnich," he said. "Then I'm going to tear down that excuse for a shelter he threw together."

What seemed like forever later, Bri was cradling Boyo in her arms, her head resting against his. She was still murmuring encouragement to him, every bone and muscle complaining in pain at the awkward position she was sitting in, when she heard the sound of the helicopter approaching. She'd have cheered, but she didn't have the energy.

Boyo had been dozing from the effects of the painkiller, but he opened his eyes and moved his head enough to look up at the sky, golden now with the setting sun.

"Yes, baby," she said, ruffling his wiry coat. "It's the boss. He's come to take you home." For the first time, Boyo whined, but it had a happy sound to it.

Bri watched as the copter came into sight, then stopped to hover overhead. She saw the line with the rescue basket attached, Hawk in a harness, clinging to the line as it slowly dropped to the ground. Tanner was waiting to catch it.

Between them, Tanner and Hawk lifted an unconscious Minnich into the basket and motioned to have it hauled up. Before it was off the ground, Hawk was striding to where Bri sat cradling his wounded pet.

"So, then, laddie, you took a bullet for my friends, did you?" Hawk said, the contrived Scottish burr failing to conceal the concern in his tone.

At the sound of Hawk's voice, Boyo's tail began thumping against the ground. Bri blinked against the mist stinging her eyes.

Hawk dropped to one knee as another basket was lowered from the copter. "Okay, fella," he said, sliding his arms under the dog. "Grit your teeth, 'cause I'm gonna lift you." Slowly, very carefully, he rose to his feet. Cradling Boyo in his arms like a child, he carried him to where Tanner waited.

Gritting her own teeth, grunting, swearing to herself, Bri pushed herself upright and, moving stiffly, followed at Hawk's heels. She saw Tanner remove a small cooler from the basket as Hawk approached.

After Boyo was settled into the blanket-padded basket, Hawk turned to Bri and drew her into his arms for a strong hug. "Thanks for taking care of him, Brianna," he said in a suspiciously choked voice.

She stepped back to look at him with worried eyes. "Will he be all right, do you think?"

He gave her a nod and a shaky smile. "He's a tough one. He'll live to see his pups."

"But…" she began, confused by his remark.

"Gotta go," he said, turning to shake Tanner's hand, then pull him into a quick hug. "Thanks, my friend."

"Anytime, buddy." Tanner stepped back. Hawk fastened himself into the harness and grabbed the line, and he and the basket disappeared inside the copter.

The hunt was over.

Bri watched until the rescue helicopter was out of sight. When she looked around the area, she saw Tanner had not only cleared away the makeshift camp but had set up their domed tent and brought the horses from where they had left them.

"I see you were busy while waiting for the helicopter," she said, feeling a twinge at having not helped him. "I'm sorry I wasn't any help…." she began.

He gave a sharp shake of his head. "I didn't need any help. Boyo did."

That quick, at just the mention of the dog's name, Bri got all misty-eyed again. Just as quickly she felt Tanner's arm around her, pulling her toward him in a comforting embrace.

"Don't worry, Bri. He'll be fine. He's one tough dog. Now…" He slanted her a grin and wiggled his brows at the cooler Hawk had brought. "Let's eat."

"Hawk brought us supper?"

He nodded. "I guess he figured we'd be tired of trail grub by now."

"And he was right. What did he bring?" she asked, suddenly ravenous.

Tanner began withdrawing items from the cooler. "Chili…French bread…and real brewed coffee."

Bri sighed. "Be still my heart."

"And he even packed desert," he said, pulling out brownies.

"Wonderful," she replied, her mouth nearly watering.

As evening was nearly upon them, chilling the air, Tanner built a small fire inside a ring of stones and they sat to eat.

"Getting chilly?" he asked, when he saw her shiver. Without waiting for her reply, he draped her jacket around her shoulders.

Sighing with gratitude from the warmth of the jacket and the fire, she smiled her thanks.

Everything tasted delicious, warming her inside as the fire and her jacket kept her warm outside. Bri silently thanked Hawk for everything, sighing in contentment over her second cup of coffee.

"Feel better now?"

"Much, thank you," she answered. She stared into the fire letting her mind wander back to the action earlier that day. "Tanner, Hawk said something about Boyo living to see his pups," she said. "What did he mean?"

"Just what he said. Hawk has a friend, a breeder

of wolfhounds, and every so often he'll agree to her plea for him to bring Boyo to impregnate one of the bitches she feels is champion-producing material. His pups are due any day now."

Bri smiled, the first one since they had sighted Minnich. "I bet they'll be beautiful."

"So far, they all have been, and some of them have become champions." He gave her an encouraging grin. "And I'm sure Hawk's right—Boyo will live to see his litter and many others."

Bri was quiet a moment, not sure she wanted to know or even cared, but she finally asked, "And Minnich?"

Tanner's features went hard. "Oh, he'll live to face a jury." He was silent a moment before he added, "And by the way, we *both* got him. I hit him in the thigh, you got him in the shoulder. Now forget him. He's not worth one more moment of your thoughts."

"Right." Bri nodded, swallowing against a sudden tightness in her throat, blinking against a sharp stinging in her eyes. "I'm beat. Let's get this stuff cleared away so I can turn in."

"Go," he ordered. "I'll do it." He arched a brow. "Would you like me to warm some water so you can have a—" he grinned "—cup bath?"

"Oh, that would be wonderful, Tanner. Thank you." She heaved herself up off the log.

He waved her away. "Go, get ready, I'll be with you in a few minutes."

She was waiting for him in the tent, stripped

naked except for a towel she had wrapped around her shivering body. Tanner stepped into the tent to hand her the bigmouthed thermos and cup.

"Take your time," he said, lifting the flap to leave her alone. "I'm going to clean up at the stream."

Although it was big for a thermos lid, bathing from it was more than a little difficult. Bri managed, at least enough to make her feel reasonably clean again. Though she was cold, she relished the feel of the water as the cupful sluiced down her body. She imagined it washing away not only the grime but the horror she had seen that day. The pain that she had endured while watching her sister suffer. It was over now, but somehow she couldn't get it out of her system.

When the thermos was empty, she dried and dressed in another pair of long johns and socks she'd stuffed into her pack. She had just exited the tent when Tanner came back to camp.

"Better?" He was close enough for his breath to ruffle her hair.

"Yes." She spoke true, to a point. Her body and clothes were clean, but she was tired and emotionally exhausted. Maybe that's why the dam burst.

Tears welled in her eyes. Bri could no longer hold them at bay, nor the sobs clawing at her throat.

Turning away from him, she ran into the tent, and scrambled under the cover. Unable to stem the tide, she wept like a heartbroken child.

"Hey, Brianna, what's this?" Concern deepening

his voice, Tanner crawled into the sleeping bag next to her, turning her into his arms. "Honey, it's over now," he murmured, drawing her protectively closer to him. "Why are you crying?"

"I was thinking of Dani—" she sobbed. "Now maybe she'll unlock her bedroom door and come join the family again for meals, start living again."

"I'm sure she will." Tanner stroked her hair as he tried to reassure her. "Maybe you and your parents can even talk her into seeking professional help."

Bri nodded, the tears clogging her throat and blocking her voice. In his arms she wept and wept, for what seemed an eternity.

When the emotional storm passed and her tears had subsided, Bri managed, "Thank you." She took Tanner's hankie and wiped her eyes and cheeks.

"You're welcome," he said.

She sighed. "Now I've got your shirt wet."

"It'll dry," he whispered near her ear, softly, almost affectionately. "Now go to sleep."

"One more thing." She tilted her head up. He drew back to stare at her face with those heart-meltingly gentle eyes. "Since the hunt's over, do we have to get up at the crack of dawn tomorrow morning?"

He laughed. "No, sweetheart, we don't. You may sleep in an hour or so longer. But we need enough time to eat and collect our personal gear. Hawk said there would be a helicopter arriving to pick us up around midmorning."

"But what about the horses?"

"Wrangler friends of Hawk's will be along to take care of the animals and bring them in."

"Oh, okay." She yawned, so bone-tired now that she'd let out her suppressed emotions.

Tanner lowered his head to softly press his mouth to hers in a sweet good-night kiss.

But, as it had the night before, the kiss deepened immediately, setting off a firestorm of passion between them. Suddenly Bri was wide-awake, grasping his hair to pull him closer to her, returning his kiss with everything in her.

When he could, Tanner said, "Brianna, you're tired. Are you sure you want—"

"Yes, I want," she said, running her hands over his shoulders, down his already heaving chest. "I want your kiss, your body, all of you."

"And I want you the same way," Tanner muttered in a half growl of need.

After some hurried shuffling around, their clothes were gone, heaped on the tent floor on either side of them. Tanner was kissing her, her lips, her face, her breasts and lower. He kissed at the juncture of her thighs, and she cried out with pleasure. Before her cry faded, he was inside her, increasing her pleasure to near screaming point. This time when they climaxed, they soared over the edge of ecstasy together.

"That was lovely," she murmured, curling against him. In the next moment she was sound asleep.

"*You* are lovely," Tanner whispered. Fully aware she couldn't hear him, he added, "And I love you."

* * *

The helicopter dropped them off on the helipad at Hawk's place. Bri lugged her gear to the house, eagerly waiting while Tanner unlocked the door with the key Hawk had given him. Hawk had remained in town at the animal hospital with Boyo.

The minute she stepped inside, she dropped to the floor everything but her backpack and took off for the bathroom.

"What's the hurry?" Tanner called after her. "Don't you want some lunch?"

"No." Bri kept going so had to raise her voice. "I want to soak in a tub full of hot water for hours. *Then* I want some lunch."

Tanner was laughing. She could hear him through the door of the bedroom she had slept in before. She practically tore off her dirty clothing, grabbed the one clean set of bra and panties she had left and made a dash for the bathroom.

Bri didn't soak for hours. She remained in the water only until it got cold. Then she turned on the shower to rinse off before shampooing her hair.

Feeling wonderfully clean and refreshed, she returned to the bedroom, dressed and went in search of food. After a satisfying lunch, she hit the bed. It was beginning to get dark when a light tap on the door and Tanner's voice woke her.

"Brianna? I've rustled up some supper for us. Are you hungry?"

"Starving," she answered with the sudden realization. The exercise of hot sex and emotional upheaval must have activated her appetite. "Give me five minutes."

"Take ten." Laughter danced in his voice. "It will keep."

Nine minutes later, Bri entered the kitchen dressed in socks and the wrinkled but clean blue jeans and T-shirt she had put on after her bath. "What smells so good and spicy?"

"Pasta with marinara sauce." Tanner smiled. "I poured you a glass of Chianti. Help yourself to the pasta."

The meal was delicious, the Chianti the perfect complement to the pasta. The fresh brewed coffee afterward was wonderful, and the slice of apple pie Tanner had found in the freezer and baked was just the right finisher.

"We'll leave first thing in the morning," Tanner said when they'd finished.

Bri was relieved he didn't suggest they start out that night, as she was still feeling tired and sleepy. It *had* been a long time since her last trek.

Together, they cleaned up the kitchen to the spotless condition Hawk kept it in, then shared a final glass of wine, exchanging mundane conversation until, rising and stretching, Tanner said he was ready to turn in. As Bri was every bit as ready, she washed their glasses and he dried them.

They were so tired they slept in separate beds that night.

Tanner woke her early the next morning. There was one difference, though. This time she was ready to get up, and most of the aches and stiffness were gone. They were on the road less than an hour later.

Bri was glad to be going back. At least that's what she told herself. In truth, though, with each passing mile she felt more and more deflated, depressed. It was probably the sudden release of the tension of the hunt, she reasoned. It had nothing at all to do with her leaving Tanner and very likely never seeing him again.

"You've been awful quiet," he said as they parked by the side of the road to rest and eat lunch. "Is something bothering you?"

"No." Bri shook her head. "I, uh, I've been thinking about going home."

"Oh." He was silent for a moment. "I guess you're anxious to see your sister and parents."

"Yes, of course, even though they'll have heard the news of his capture by know, I suppose."

"Yeah."

The conversation between them was less than scintillating, more like desultory. Bri had a stupid urge to cry, which didn't make a bit of sense. She was going home at last. She should be feeling elated, not darn near morose. Shouldn't she?

Their lunch finished, Tanner didn't start the SUV; he just sat there, gripping the wheel.

"I love you, you know." His voice was flat, stark with an astounding note of pain.

Bri stopped breathing. When she could take in air again, she raised her head to look at him in wonder. He was so beautiful it made her heart ache. "I love you, too, Tanner."

"It can't work." He looked and sounded sad, regretful.

Tears rushed to Bri's eyes. She had to swallow before attempting to speak. "Tanner, couldn't we find—"

He silenced her with a rough shake of his head. "No, Brianna, and you know it as well as I do. You belong back east, doing research in your quiet library. I belong out here, somewhere, wherever. I'm not going to change. I am what I do."

"Couldn't we work together?" she asked, a pleading note in her voice. "Was I such a drag on you?"

He gave her one of his gentle smiles. "No, love. I enjoyed having you along. But this was a short, fairly easy hunt. Most of them aren't. And you were aching by the time we caught him. Sometimes I'm gone weeks, not days. It simply couldn't work for us."

Tears rolled down her cheeks. "Tanner…"

"Brianna, don't. You're tearing me apart inside." He pulled her close, shutting his eyes against the pain. "I wish it could be different, but wishing won't change anything. This time with you has been wonderful, more than I probably deserve. But it's over. We live in two different worlds, and mine is too dangerous to risk hurting the woman I love."

Accepting his word as final, Bri remained still, miserable throughout the rest of the drive into Durango, with barely a word spoken between them. What more was there to say? It was late when Tanner pulled up to the Strater Hotel, where they were holding Bri's room for her.

Her throat was tight with emotion she refused to reveal to him. She grasped the door release and softly said, "Goodbye, Tanner. I'll have your check for a million dollars delivered to you tomorrow."

"I don't want it, Brianna. This one's on me."

She gave a quick shake of her head. "No. The bounty is yours. You earned it. Don't bother sending it back. Remember, my father is a banker. It would be easy for him to have it deposited into your account."

"Okay, you win."

Right. Bri wanted to weep. She didn't, though; she turned to the door. He stopped her by curling one big hand around her nape and turning her to him, claiming her mouth with his own. His kiss was deep and passionate and tasted of urgency, desperation. When he let her go, he moved back behind the wheel, his face once again carved in stone. "Goodbye, Brianna."

Bri almost stumbled out the door. Tanner's voice stopped her as her boots hit the pavement.

"Take care of yourself."

She couldn't look back at him. "You, too," she said over her shoulder and went striding for the entrance

doors. As soon as she stepped inside, she heard his
SUV drive away. Knowing he was taking her heart
with him, she kept moving, not looking back.

Eleven

Bri was back in her own apartment two days, and the pain was still unbearable. It had seeped beneath her skin, soaking her insides, drowning her in misery. She had given in to tears again when Tanner called her.

"Hi, Brianna. How are you? And how was your flight back home?"

The sound of his voice, low, intimate, even asking such innocuous questions, set her pulse thumping. "I'm fine and so was the flight," she answered, telling herself to grow up, while trying to catch her breath. "How are you, Tanner?"

"Fine."

Bri frowned at the handset. Was that all he had to say?

"That's good," she replied. What else could she say, anyway? Make an ass of herself by admitting she missed him so much she ached? What good could come of that? He'd told her a relationship between them wouldn't work.

"How is Boyo?" she asked, knowing she should have thought of the dog at once.

"He'll be fine. He's still in the hospital, but they removed the bullet, so all he has to do now is heal. And here's more good news. His pups were born yesterday morning. Seven of them."

"Lucky number. I'd love to see them. Have you?"

"No, not yet." He paused. "How is Dani?"

"Better. At least she unlocks her bedroom door and joins our parents for meals. But she doesn't go out much, and never alone."

"It'll take time." Again he paused, as if having run out of things to say.

"I know," she said. "One good thing—she has agreed to get professional help."

"That's good." He paused again. "Uh, besides wanting to know how you were doing, I called to tell you I've accepted another job."

For a second, when he said *job,* hope flared that he was referring to a regular nine-to-five kind. She should have known better, she chided herself. "Another hunt." It was not a question but a statement.

"Yes, this time in the city." He went on before

she could ask. "An embezzler suspected of having gone to ground in a rough section of L.A."

"Do you know the city well?" Bri was already worrying, and he hadn't even left yet.

"Not like I know the mountains," he admitted, adding, "but I'll find him." There was not so much as a hint of false pride or bravado in his voice, just certainty.

"I know you will." Brianna drew a deep breath. "Will you try not to get yourself hurt while you're at it?"

He laughed. "I'll work on it."

She tried laughing with him, but she couldn't push one past the tightness in her throat. She didn't want him to hunt—at least not without her along to watch his back, and having hers caressed with wonderful building passion.

"Brianna?" Concern shaded his voice at her silence.

"Yes?"

"I thought you had hung up." There was another tight, strained pause, as if he were now having trouble finding words. "I, er, I'd better hang up. I'm leaving tomorrow and I still have to pack."

"Okay. Goodbye, Tanner. Stay safe." She wanted to hold him close, keep him safe. Foolish woman.

"I'll give it my best." He hesitated, then said softly, "I miss you, Brianna."

He disconnected before she could reply. It didn't matter; she wasn't sure she could speak, anyway, not without sobbing. She stood there holding the phone, unaware of the low buzz on the line or the tears rolling down her face.

Brianna.

Tanner stood stone-still, gripping the handset. He closed his eyes against the ache throbbing through him, the need, the emptiness. He had never felt anything like the longing he was feeling for her, her laughter, the teasing light in her eyes at times, like when she was doling out her precious dark chocolate.

Damn, he thought, being in love hurt so badly, throughout his entire body, his mind, his soul.

Sighing for what could never be, he cradled the handset, telling himself to stop mooning like a kid and get his ass in gear. He had a job to do. Yet, try as he did, Tanner couldn't shake the thought that he'd miss having Brianna working right there beside him.

The following weeks were a drag for Bri. Spring and the final exams at the university came and went, along with the majority of the students. Although there were always summer students, a lot fewer than usual roamed the campus library.

Bri was bored and restless and hungry with a hollow appetite that had nothing to do with food. When not at work in the library, she worked hard at staying busy. She turned down every invitation to go out with both her women friends and several men. There was only one man who interested her, and he was off hunting a criminal, putting his life in danger. She worked real hard not to think about that.

She spent most of her free time at her parents' house, with her sister. Though improved, Dani still kept close to home and was now dreading the day she would have to testify against Jay Minnich, who had been extradited from Colorado to Pennsylvania. And even though the man was behind bars and not likely to be going anywhere soon, Dani was still afraid to go out alone, if she went out at all.

The mild weather of spring melted into the hot days of summer. While attempting to keep Dani's spirits up, Bri felt as if she were being eaten alive inside with worry over Tanner, who hadn't called again. Was he safe? Was he deliberately not calling to indicate a final break-off of their— What?— friendship? Relationship?

She cried a lot and slept little in her bed each night. And it was in the middle of one of those weepy, sleepless nights when the phone rang, startling and scaring her.

Was something wrong with her parents? Dani? Before panic could set in, Bri grabbed the handset to stare at the lighted caller ID window. It was a cell phone number, one she didn't recognize. She hesitated before answering in a cautious tone.

"Hello?"

"Brianna?" His voice was low, muffled.

"Tanner?" A full range of emotions, primarily relief, flooded through her. "Is that you?"

"Yes," he murmured. "I'm sorry to wake you."

"Oh, that doesn't matter." She didn't tell him she never slept. "Where are you? Your voice sounds strange. Are you all right?"

"Yes, yes, don't worry," he whispered. "My voice sounds strange because I have my hand cupped around the phone so no one can hear me. I'm still in L.A., in a twenty-four-hour grungy, hole-in-the-wall diner."

"What in the world are you doing there?" Even as the words poured out of her mouth, Bri knew it was a stupid question.

"I'm sure as hell not enjoying myself," he muttered. "I'm working, remember?"

"Yes, of course," she said. "Are you getting anywhere with your hunt?"

"Yeah, I'm practically on this crook's ass," he answered with soft satisfaction. "But that isn't why I called. You'll be receiving a delivery sometime tomorrow. Since it's Saturday, I hope you'll be home."

"A delivery?" Bri frowned. "I'll stay home until it arrives, but what is it?"

"I don't have time to go into it now." His voice was lower, rushed. "There's a letter with it that will explain everything. I gotta go now."

"Okay, goodbye." She swallowed a need to protest. "Please take care."

"Always." His voice dropped to barely a whisper. "Goodbye, Brianna." There came a pause, making her think he had disconnected, then with a sigh he said, "I miss you, Brianna. I love you." A click. He was gone.

I love you.

Throughout what was left of the darkness, Bri held his words close, warming her heart, even as fear for his safety chilled every bone in her body. By first light she had made a decision. Like it or not—and Tanner very likely wouldn't like it—she was going back to Durango, to him, to be his partner in everything.

Tanner claimed to love her, and she knew she was in love with him. So his work was dangerous. Bri knew she could deal with the danger so long as she was beside him, watching his back.

Rising with the summer sun, Bri began getting her things together, as many of her things that would fit in her car. She could send for the rest later. She decided she would keep the apartment for visits home. No, her home would be wherever Tanner was. She'd keep the place for visits to her parents and Dani.

By late morning her small living room was littered with suitcases, hunting gear and bags full of things she couldn't fit into her cases. Gazing around her, Bri was wondering how she had ever collected so much stuff when the doorbell rang.

The delivery Tanner had told her to expect. In her flurry of activity, she had completely forgotten. She went to the door, opened it and stood, stunned, staring at the uniformed delivery man.

What in the…? Her thoughts scattered. In one hand he held the handle to an animal carrier. In the other a large shipping bag.

"Ms. Stewart?"

She nodded, numb with confusion. She could see something wriggling through the openings in the carrier. The deliveryman stepped inside, set both items on the floor and thrust a small clipboard at her.

"I'll need your signature, ma'am."

Bri signed on the line, managed a smile and a murmured "Thank you" and closed the door behind him.

Carefully she picked up the carrier, for the first time noticing an envelope taped to one side. She'd get to the letter later, Bri thought, but first she peeked into the opening and exhaled a soft, "Ooh. Hello, there, little one."

The puppy inside gave a low whine, while the tail wagged in excitement. Though the dog didn't look much like him, Bri knew it was one of Boyo's litter, and it was adorable.

Setting the carrier back down on the floor, Bri tore the envelope from the side, ripped it open and began reading the letter from Tanner.

Brianna, this pup is not for you. I wrote this note before leaving for L.A. and gave it to Hawk, along with instructions. I'm sure you knew at once the pup is one of Boyo's. She was the runt of the litter. I asked Hawk to take Boyo to see his puppies as soon as he was well and to pick out one of the pups. Hawk called to tell me he had done so, and Boyo had immediately singled out the little female runt. She has had her shots, but she doesn't have a name. She is a gift for Dani—and her right to name. Inside the other package Dani will find food and supplies to get started. Also, there's a booklet with information about the breed.

Tell Dani she doesn't need to fear so long as the pup is with her. As you know, the pup will grow—not quite as tall as Boyo but tall enough. She will be loving, loyal and willing to give her own life for her mistress…as you know from experience.

Love, Tanner

Tears were running down Bri's cheeks by the time she finished his letter. Oh, how she loved this kind, compassionate, wonderful, sexy, beautiful and at times arrogant man.

Wiping her eyes with her fingers, Bri grabbed her purse, picked up the carrier and shipping bag and dashed out of the apartment.

Ten minutes later, she burst into her parents' home. Her mother was coming down the stairs, surprise obvious in her expression. "Bri, what's your hurry?"

"Dani," she answered. "Where's Dani?"

"Out by the pool, but— What do you have

there?" she called after Bri as she headed for the sliding door leading to the patio and pool area.

"Come, come," Bri called back, excitement singing on her voice. "Come see."

At Bri's hurried approach, Dani looked as puzzled as their mother. "Bri, what—" That was as far as she got.

"Look," Bri said, holding the carrier out to her. "This is for you."

"For me? But... Oh, my heavens! Bri, it's a puppy."

"I know." Bri laughed. "It's *your* puppy." As Dani began fiddling with the latch on the door of the carrier, Bri quickly added, "Wait. Before you take her out, I have this for you." She handed over the letter.

Dani began to read aloud. It wasn't long before she was blinking against a sting of tears. It didn't matter, because both Bri and their mother were also misty-eyed.

"Oh, Bri, what a thoughtful gift. Tanner sounds like a wonderful man."

"He is...." Bri's throat was so tight she could hardly get the words out. "Now you can take her out. And don't forget—you must find a name for her."

Dani carefully drew the dog from the carrier. "Oh, she's beautiful!" She cradled the wiggly ball of fur close to her, laughing when the puppy tried to shower every inch of her face with kisses.

Laughing with sheer delight for the first time since her shattering ordeal, Dani looked up at Bri and their mother. "I don't have to think about naming her," she said, laughing and crying at the same time. "Just look at her. What else could I name her but Beauty."

"Perfect." Bri laughed. "Now hand her over and let me get some of those kisses."

Bri stayed at her parents' for dinner. Over an impeccable meal, with Dani at her side, she explained what she planned to do.

There were some arguments that her plan was hasty and there was more than a little concern from her parents. Though she didn't say a word, Dani smiled and gave her sister a thumbs-up.

In the end, of course, Bri held firm. Early the next morning she stashed all her packed stuff in the trunk and backseat of her car and headed west.

Bri was going on a manhunt of her own.

It was late afternoon when Bri pulled her car into Durango after what seemed like forever on the road. Before signing in at the Strater Hotel, as she had done previously, she pulled into the first parking space she came across, dug her cell phone from her cavernous handbag and dialed Tanner's apartment number. To her surprise, he answered on the second ring.

"Wolfe."

Relief at knowing he was back safe washed through her. "Hello, Wolfe, how are you?"

"Brianna!" Could that be the sound of happiness she detected in his voice? "You got my message?"

Her brows wrinkled. "What message?"

"I called not ten minutes after I got home yesterday and I left a message on your answering machine."

Bri groaned. She had checked her home phone for messages every day except yesterday and today. "No, I didn't get it. I, er, I'm not at home, Tanner."

"Where are you, then?" His tone now held a definite edge. Where the heck did he suspect she might be, and with whom?

"I'm right here in Durango, just a short distance from your apartment."

He was silent for a moment. "Then get the hell here now. You hear me?"

She smiled. "Yes, Tanner, I hear you. I'll be there in a few minutes."

"You'd better be."

Her smile widened into a grin. He'd actually growled at her, like the animal whose name he bore.

Bri took only two things with her from the car. She was holding one of them in each hand when she rang his doorbell. It swung open at once, and she burst out laughing at the sight that met her eyes.

Tanner stood with one shoulder propped against the door frame, his long, shiny hair draping his shoulders. In one hand he held a bag of dark chocolate—purple-wrapped Hershey's Kisses. In the other he held the glittery gold cloth strips of the sandals she had worn the day he'd picked her up.

"Hi." He grinned at her astonished expression and stepped back, allowing her to enter.

"Where did you find them?" she asked. "I've been tearing my closet apart looking for them."

"They were stuffed under the front seat of the SUV." He laughed. "If you'll recall, you tossed them in the back when you put on your boots."

"Thank you for finding them. They're one of my favorite pairs."

"Mine, too." He eyed her hands. "And what have you got there?" He inclined his head, indicating the folded material she held in one hand and the large, round, old-fashioned hatbox in the other.

Bri was so busy drinking in the sight of him she had forgotten the items she held. "This, I believe, is yours." She handed over the folded material, which he couldn't help but recognize as his own hankie he had given her on their last night of the hunt.

"And this," she said, handing the box to him, "is a present from me to you."

He looked puzzled. "A present for me? Why would you buy me a ladies' hatbox from a bygone day?"

She gave him a look and an impatient sigh. "Open the box and look for yourself, Tanner."

Dumping the sandals, the bag of candy and his snow-white, neatly pressed hankie into her arms, he took the box and set it on the sofa. He untied the frayed laces holding the lid on and gave her a wary look.

"Nothing's going to jump out at me?"

"Oh, good grief, Tanner!" Bri shook her head. "You're a big, tough hunter. Open the silly box."

Laughing, he lifted the lid. His laughter gave way to an expression of wonder. Slowly, carefully, he lifted the buff-colored Stetson from the box. "Brianna... Why?"

"That one doesn't have a bullet hole in it." She gave him a teasing grin. "I bought myself one exactly like it."

"You're something," he said, plopping the hat on his head before pulling her into his arms and thanking her with a scorching kiss.

They broke apart for one reason— to breathe. When Tanner lowered his head to her once more, Bri raised a trembling hand to his chest to hold him back.

She drew a deep breath. "Tanner, wait. We've got to talk."

"We can talk later." He moved forward, backing her against the wall. "But first we've got more important things to do."

"No." She shook her head, bringing her other hand up to keep him a few inches from her. "No, Tanner. I didn't come here for sex." She gave a half laugh, qualifying her statement with, "At least not *only* for sex."

His eyes narrowed. "Okay, what do you want?"

"You."

"But you just said—"

"All of you, dammit!" She glared into those glittering eyes. "I want to be your partner…in every aspect of your life. In marriage, in work—and I do mean in the hunt—and, yes, sex."

Arching a brow, Tanner took on that austere statue-of-a-saint expression.

She arched a brow right back at him, although she couldn't match him for austerity. "And don't give me that look. It doesn't impress or intimidate me. Oh, Tanner," she murmured, lifting one hand to caress his face. "I love you. I want to be with you."

"It can't work," he said, shaking his head but covering his hand over hers to keep it where it was. "You'd be a nervous wreck sitting at home, waiting and worrying about me. And some jobs require me to be away for weeks. Hell, I was away over a month in L.A."

"You're not listening, Tanner." She scowled at him. "I said I want to be with you in every aspect." She slid her fingers slowly down his cheek, smiling as his tight expression softened. "That includes your hunts. You need someone to cover your back, and I intend to be that someone."

"You do, do you?" He moved closer, his body pressing into hers. "A ring on your finger and one through my nose, huh?"

"Oh, don't be silly," she said, smiling as she outlined his lips with her fingertip. "Nose rings are so yesterday." She gasped as he caught her finger between his teeth and sucked it into his mouth. With his body pressed tightly against her, she could feel his readiness for her and knew he could feel her shivery response. Time to bring out her last weapon.

"Tanner, I love you. And I'll continue to love you whether you're here or on a hunt. I would rather die with you on a hunt than live without you near me."

"You don't play fair," he murmured, dipping his head to taste her neck.

"Not when I'm playing for such high stakes." She arched her body into his, feeling the hard fullness of him against her. "Give me an answer now or I swear I'll be out of here in a shot."

"No, you won't." He raised his head a bit to smile at her.

"No," she admitted, snaking her arms around his neck to get closer still. "I won't."

He laughed. "You're still a little nuts, but I like you that way. Brianna, my love, will you marry me...and cover my back on our hunts?"

"Oh, Tanner, yes, yes, yes." She planted a swift, hard kiss on his smiling lips. When he reached for the buttons on her shirt, she caught his hand, held it still. "Wait, there's one more thing."

Tanner groaned. "Brianna, you're killing me here. I'm ready to go up in flames."

"Oh, my, we can't have that," she actually cooed.

"Then what is it?" He sounded like a man at the end of his rope.

"Could we please use a bed this time?"

Tanner roared with laughter. Sweeping her up into his arms, he strode toward the short hall to his bedroom.

"Oh, sweetheart, have I got a bed for you."

It was a king-size. Just perfect for two nutty lovers.

Tanner made love to Brianna with his hat on.

* * * * *

Silhouette® Romantic Suspense
keeps getting hotter!
Turn the page for a sneak preview of
Wendy Rosnau's latest SPY GAMES *title*
SLEEPING WITH DANGER

Available November 2007

Silhouette® Romantic Suspense—
Sparked by Danger, Fueled by Passion!

Melita had been expecting a chaste quick kiss of the generic variety. But this kiss with Sully was the kind that sparked a dying flame to life. The kind of kiss you can't plan for. The kind of kiss memories are built on.

The memory of her murdered lover, Nemo, came to her then and she made a starved little noise in the back of her throat. She raised her arms and threaded her fingers through Sully's hair, pulled him closer. Felt his body settle, then melt into her.

In that instant her hunger for him grew, and his for her. She pressed herself to him with more urgency, and he responded in kind.

Melita came out of her kiss-induced memory of Nemo with a start. "Wait a minute." She pushed Sully away from her. "You bastard!"

She spit two nasty words at him in Greek, then wiped his kiss from her lips.

"I thought you deserved some solid proof that I'm still in one piece." He started for the door. "The clock's ticking, honey. Come on, let's get out of here."

"That's it? You sucker me into kissing you, and that's all you have to say?"

"I'm sorry. How's that?"

He didn't sound sorry in the least. "You're—"

"Getting out of this godforsaken prison cell. Stop whining and let's go."

"Not if I was being shot at sunrise. Go. You deserve whatever you get if you walk out that door."

He turned back. "Freedom is what I'm going to get."

"A second of freedom before the guards in the hall shoot you." She jammed her hands on her hips. "And to think I was worried about you."

"If you're staying behind, it's no skin off my ass."

"Wait! What about our deal?"

"You just said you're not coming. Make up your mind."

"Have you forgotten we need a boat?"

"How could I? You keep harping on it."

"I'm not going without a boat. And those guards

out there aren't going to just let you walk out of here. You need me and we need a plan."

"I already have a plan. I'm getting out of here. That's the plan."

"I should have realized that you never intended to take me with you from the very beginning. You're a liar and a coward."

Of everything she had read, there was nothing in Sully Paxton's file that hinted he was a coward, but it was the one word that seemed to register in that one track mind of his. The look he nailed her with a second later was pure venom.

He came at her so quickly she didn't have time to get out of his way. "You know I'm not a coward."

"Prove it. Give me until dawn. I need one more night to put everything in place before we leave the island."

"You're asking me to stay in this cell one more night...and trust you?"

"Yes."

He snorted. "Yesterday you knew they were planning to harm me, but instead of doing something about it you went to bed and never gave me a second thought. Suppose tonight you do the same. By tomorrow I might damn well be in my grave."

"Okay, I screwed up. I won't do it again." Melita sucked in a ragged breath. "I can't leave this minute. Dawn, Sully. Wait until dawn." When he looked as if he was about to say no, she pleaded, "Please, wait for me."

"You're asking a lot. The door's open now. I would be a fool to hang around here and trust that you'll be back."

"What you can trust is that I want off this island as badly as you do, and you're my only hope."

"I must be crazy."

"Is that a yes?"

"Dammit!" He turned his back on her. Swore twice more.

"You won't be sorry."

He turned around. "I already am. How about we seal this new deal?"

He was staring at her lips. Suddenly Melita knew what he expected. "We already sealed it."

"One more. You enjoyed it. Admit it."

"I enjoyed it because I was kissing someone else."

He laughed. "That's a good one."

"It's true. It might have been your lips, but it wasn't you I was kissing."

"If that's your excuse for wanting to kiss me, then—"

"I was kissing Nemo."

"What's a nemo?"

Melita gave Sully a look that clearly told him that he was trespassing on sacred ground. She was about to enforce it with a warning when a voice in the hall jerked them both to attention.

She bolted away from the wall. "Get back in bed. Hurry. I'll be here before dawn."

She didn't reach the door before he snagged her

arm, pulled her up against him and planted a kiss on her lips that took her completely by surprise.

When he released her, he said, "If you're confused about who just kissed you, the name's Sully. I'll be here waiting at dawn. Don't be late."

® HARLEQUIN®

Mediterranean
NIGHTS™

*Not everything is above board
on Alexandra's Dream!*

*Enjoy plenty of secrets, drama and sensuality
in the latest from Mediterranean Nights.*

Coming in November 2007...

BELOW DECK

by

Dorien Kelly

Determined to protect her young son,
widow Mei Lin Wang keeps him hidden
aboard *Alexandra's Dream* under cover of
her job. But life gets extremely complicated
when the ship's security officer, Gideon Dayan,
is piqued by the mystery surrounding this
beautiful, haunted woman....

REQUEST YOUR FREE BOOKS!

2 FREE NOVELS
PLUS 2
FREE GIFTS!

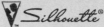

Silhouette®

Desire®

Passionate, Powerful, Provocative!

YES! Please send me 2 FREE Silhouette Desire® novels and my 2 FREE gifts. After receiving them, if I don't wish to receive any more books, I can return the shipping statement marked "cancel." If I don't cancel, I will receive 6 brand-new novels every month and be billed just $3.80 per book in the U.S., or $4.47 per book in Canada, plus 25¢ shipping and handling per book and applicable taxes, if any*. That's a savings of almost 15% off the cover price! I understand that accepting the 2 free books and gifts places me under no obligation to buy anything. I can always return a shipment and cancel at any time. Even if I never buy another book from Silhouette, the two free books and gifts are mine to keep forever.

225 SDN EEXJ   326 SDN EEXU

Name	(PLEASE PRINT)

Address	Apt.

City	State/Prov.	Zip/Postal Code

Signature (if under 18, a parent or guardian must sign)

Mail to the **Silhouette Reader Service™:**
IN U.S.A.: P.O. Box 1867, Buffalo, NY 14240-1867
IN CANADA: P.O. Box 609, Fort Erie, Ontario L2A 5X3

Not valid to current Silhouette Desire subscribers.

Want to try two free books from another line?
Call 1-800-873-8635 or visit www.morefreebooks.com.

* Terms and prices subject to change without notice. NY residents add applicable sales tax. Canadian residents will be charged applicable provincial taxes and GST. This offer is limited to one order per household. All orders subject to approval. Credit or debit balances in a customer's account(s) may be offset by any other outstanding balance owed by or to the customer. Please allow 4 to 6 weeks for delivery.

Your Privacy: Silhouette is committed to protecting your privacy. Our Privacy Policy is available online at www.eHarlequin.com or upon request from the Reader Service. From time to time we make our lists of customers available to reputable firms who may have a product or service of interest to you. If you would prefer we not share your name and address, please check here. ☐

SDES07

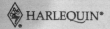

EVERLASTING LOVE ™

Every great love has a story to tell ™

Charlie fell in love with Rose Kaufman
before he even met her, through stories her
husband, Joe, used to tell. When Joe is killed
in the trenches, Charlie helps Rose through
her grief and they make a new life together.
But for Charlie, a question remains—can
love be as true the second time around?
Only one woman can answer that....

Look for

*The Soldier and
the Rose*

by
Linda Barrett

Available November wherever you buy books.

HEL65421

COMING NEXT MONTH

#1831 SECRETS OF THE TYCOON'S BRIDE—
Emilie Rose
The Garrisons
This playboy needs a wife and deems his accountant the perfect bride-to-be…until her scandalous past is revealed.

#1832 SOLD INTO MARRIAGE—Ann Major
Can a wealthy Texan stick to his end of the bargain when he beds the very woman he's vowed to blackmail?

#1833 CHRISTMAS IN HIS ROYAL BED—Heidi Betts
A scorned debutante discovers that the prince who hired her is the same man who wants to make her his royal mistress.

#1834 PLAYBOY'S RUTHLESS PAYBACK—
Laura Wright
No Ring Required
His plan for revenge meant seducing his rival's innocent daughter. But *is* she as innocent as he thinks?

#1835 THE DESERT BRIDE OF AL ZAYED—
Tessa Radley
Billionaire Heirs
She decided her secret marriage to the sheik must end…just as he declared the time has come to produce his heir.

#1836 THE BILLIONAIRE WHO BOUGHT CHRISTMAS—
Barbara Dunlop
To save his family's fortune, the billionaire tricked his grandfather's gold-digging fiancée into marriage. Now he discovers he's wed the wrong woman!

SDCNM1007